Tom & Polly,

We are so grateful for your
friendship. I hope you
enjoy the book!

May the Lord bless
you and keep you,

For my Wife...

Who is the inspiration for all that is romantic in me.

# The Cowboy and the Storm

The Cowboy and the Storm©2008 Kirk Mann

Chapter One

Leaving home

It was hot that July, hotter than any summer he could remember in his twenty three years on the family ranch in west Texas. To prove the point, Grandpa Bean had boiled an egg on the tin of the chicken coop earlier in the day and laughed all the way into their old white house. It was that humid sticky heat which even a north wind won't forgive. Maybe it was the mixture of the weather and his decision that James Montgomery was yet to share with his family that was causing his stomach to churn. For he felt as if he allowed it, the nervous feelings would overtake him with sickness. He had decided to leave the ranch and hire on with a large outfit just outside of Lubbock. He wanted to make it on his own steam and one day manage his own ranch. The decision was easy to make, but explaining the decision is what had him twisted up. He stood at the east fence pretending to watch the new calves play as he prepared his words carefully.

"Well...son," his father said as he crossed his arms over the fence next to his son.

He looked at his dad with some surprise; he didn't hear him walk up. "Yes, sir," he managed.

"I reckon you aim to tell us something about your going today," his father continued plainly.

James stood there looking in astonishment and then affection, because he should have known his father would know. He was the kind of man that didn't say much, because he was as careful with his words as he was his family. If you happened upon him you might mistake him for simple, since there was nothing but humility in his manner. He was far from simple and had managed to build a twenty head cattle farm into a two hundred head thriving ranch.

James continued to pretend to watch the calves play, "How long have you known?"

"Aww long enough, I suppose," his father turned to look at his son, still leaning against the fence.

"Dad, I think it's time I made my own way." He took his hat off and moved it around in his hands as he turned to look at his dad.

"James, I have watched you grow into a fine man and I have taught you all I know about ranchin," his dad put his strong hand on his son's shoulder. "This will always be your home and you're welcome back any time."

James stuck out his hand for his dad to shake, which his dad just disregarded and hugged his son.

"Does mama know?" James whispered in his father's ear as they embraced.

His dad grinned, and pulled himself back

holding his son by the shoulders, "Well…. Son, I tell ya, sometimes even a good horse will pitch."

James just smiled. That was his dad's way of saying it wasn't going to be that easy. About that time the dinner bell rang and both men started to head towards the house. After washing up the men came to the table which Grandpa Bean had already beat them to. James' mama was busy putting food on the table as she stuck out her cheek for James to kiss. Both men put their cowboy hats bottom side up on the bench next to the table and sat down just as his mama finished with the setting.

As they all took each other's hands, his dad asked his grandpa, "Dad, you want to say grace?"

"Well, of course son," Grandpa Bean cleared his throat and then began. "Dear Heavenly Father, we come to you as simple folk grateful for another day, thank you for this food that is before us and please bless the hands that prepared it. In Jesus name Amen." Grandpa Bean was never one to say much either.

James looked around the table and soaked in the view that he knew he was going to miss. He watched as Grandpa Bean moved his peas into his mashed potatoes and he smiled as his mother straightened her silverware. He looked to his dad who was looking back at him with that 'alright boy get on with it' look.

James swallowed, "Mama."

"Yes son?" She raised her deep blue eyes to look at him.

James placed his hands in his lap and looked directly at her, "I have decided it is time for me to leave the ranch and make something on my own."

His mother sat there. She looked from him to the table. She straightened her silverware again.

"Where will you go?" His mother asked still

staring at the table.

"I have been accepted with the Triple 7 ranch outside of Lubbock. I was told by Arthur Murphy with my experience I will be a foreman in training," James continued.

At this statement his mother turned to look at his dad, looking for his approval of this outfit. His dad gave a slight nod and she gave her attention back to her son.

"When do you leave?" She asked in a level tone.

James took a deep breath. "Tomorrow morning," he breathed out.

Her eyes went wide for a moment and James could tell she was controlling herself. She was cut from the kind of cloth that was part silk and part steel.

She took a long steady breath and continued, "Have you prayed about this?"

"Yes ma'am. I feel God has his hand on this," James said in a quiet, assertive voice.

"You will need lunch for the road," his mom stated as she stood up, kissed James on the forehead and went into the kitchen. James watched his mother for a moment and then realized she had gotten up to hide her emotion. She loved her son dearly, however she knew he was a man now and wouldn't dare compromise his convictions. James turned back to his food as the other men already had. They all ate in silence.

The next morning came early; James had trouble sleeping because he was setting out on the unknown. He awoke to the sound of his mama banging pans, no doubt preparing breakfast and more food for his trip. The sun hadn't peeked yet over the flat horizon as he came from his room, he noticed his dad standing on the front porch just outside the screen door. James opened the door and in the quiet of the morning the squeaking of the springs made quite the sound. His dad's back was to him as he just looked out at the pink and purple precession to the sun. James took his queue and just stood there with his father in peaceful silence. After a few moments his dad reached over and slapped money into James' hand.

"Dad, I...I can't."

His Dad's grip was as solid as rock, but his eyes were glazed with water, "You will, boy. And I ain't going to hear nothing else about it."

James fought back the emotion, "Thanks dad," and slid the money into his jeans pocket.

"I wouldn't have it any other way," his dad stated as he walked into the house for breakfast. Mama had already finished setting the table and was waiting patiently as Grandpa Bean made small talk.

After breakfast James packed his things into his old blue Chevy pickup his dad had given him when he turned sixteen. He attached the horse trailer he had won at the state fair rodeo in the bull dogging competition last year. He made his way to the horse coral, taking the trip a little slower than usual breathing in the smells of home. As he reached the coral, he spotted his horse Blue Bonnet eating feed his dad had somehow already put out. He had owned Blue Bonnet for two years now. She was a beautiful dark brown mare. James made a clicking noise and the horse immediately came to him. He lead her out to the trailer and noticed his family on the porch just standing there watching him. This was going to be hard and he knew it. He closed the latch on the trailer and locked it down. Then he made his way towards the porch. He hugged his dad and Grandpa Bean, and then his mama.

His mama held on to him. "May the Lord bless you and keep you," her voice quaked.

James pulled his head back to look at her. "I

love you, Mama, I'll be back for Thanksgiving," he said, holding back the quiver in his voice.

James gave her one more quick squeeze, turned and got into his truck. He waved to them all as he started down the old dirt driveway.

*"This is it,"* he thought, *"Triple 7, here I come."*

Chapter 2

Meeting the Storm

She finished her morning devotion and headed for breakfast with her parents at the kitchen table. Dad had the paper out shaking his head at how crazy the world is. Mom was sitting next to him looking at a Better Homes and Garden magazine and eating a breakfast bar. Susan grabbed some milk and cereal and sat down with them. Her movement brought her parents reading to a halt.

"Busy day today, Honey?" Her Father put down his paper and focused on her.

Susan pressed her cereal down into the milk, "It looks that way. I have three dog vaccinations, a sick goat that probably ate string off a hay bale, and then I am heading out to the Triple 7 ranch to doctor a few of their horses."

"Any cute cowboys out that way?" Her mother mused still looking at her dream garden of roses and tulips.

"Oh, mom... You know I don't go for those cowboy types. I need to find a man like dad," she stated plainly as she patted her dad's arm.

Her dad shook his head and took her hand, "You know, Honey, I wasn't always a preacher."

"I know, but cowboys are rough necks that don't have a clue about how to treat a woman."

Her mom closed the magazine and looked at Susan with concern, "Wow, so you've decided it isn't even possible to fall for a cowboy, is that right?"

Susan looked from her mom and dad, "Well... I know with God all things are possible, but I sure doubt it," and continued eating.

Her mom took her hand and looked at her

15

seriously. When her mother did this Susan knew it was time to stop kidding around and listen.

"You know Susan, His ways are not our ways and you must keep your heart open to what God has for you, even if it doesn't fit in your specified criteria."

"I will, Mom. I will," She put her bowl in the sink, kissed her dad on the cheek and was off to work.

She arrived at the Lubbock Animal Clinic just before 8 o'clock; it was a very clean and white building both inside and out. There were already two pet owners waiting on her. She smiled, unlocked the door and ushered them in. It was one of those days where she had rather put the pet owners on the table than the pets, because the owners were being just downright silly. The first dog owner almost fainted when she gave the dog his shots. The second insisted that his dog was depressed from watching television.

When she finished with the dogs and the goat, she packed up her large animal med kit and headed out to the Triple 7 Ranch. She was driving her little red Ford Ranger that she loved because she could haul all of her needed equipment and still get pretty good gas mileage.

As she drove she began to go over the conversation she had with her parents earlier in the day. She was twenty-five now and had never had a serious relationship.

*"Was she destined to be an old maid? Had she passed up good men because they didn't fit into her specified criteria?"* She wondered.

As she was pondering these life questions, the backend of her truck began to pull right and she heard a repetitive thumping sound. She pulled to the side of the dirt road and was dismayed to find she had a flat tire.

She opened her cell phone that showed no

signal and closed it in frustration. She took heart, however, because her daddy had showed her how to change a tire and she was a very good student. She got the tire iron out to loosen the tire nuts and quickly came to the hard realization that the guys at the automotive shop in town had used an air socket gun to tighten the bolts. Try as she might she couldn't break them loose, so she plopped down next to her truck with a deep sigh. This was an old farm road and it could be hours before someone came by. Susan was a good five miles from the Triple 7 ranch. She was contemplating walking to the ranch when in the distance she saw the dust of a truck coming.

James had just finished his lunch his mama had packed for him when he noticed a little red truck up ahead. He slowed down and as he got closer he saw a woman stand to her feet. He slowed his truck to a stop about a car link behind the woman's truck and hopped out. She had spotted his horse trailer and figured he was on his way to the Triple 7, so she made her way towards him.

Before he really looked at her James asked, "You need some help?"

"Yes, if you don't mind," came a soft reply.

At this, James really looked at her. She was hands down the most beautiful woman he had ever seen. She had long dark brown curly hair and big brown eyes that complimented her gentle features. He was so taken with his first sight of her that he forgot to say anything else for a moment. Susan watched as this tall, broad shouldered, brown headed cowboy just stood there looking at her with piercing blue eyes.

She thought to herself, "*Now he would be good looking if he wasn't the cowboy type.*"

"The nuts on my tire are on too tight. Do you think you can break them loose?" She pointed to her truck.

James smiled recovering his composer, "Yes, ma'am, I think I can manage."

He walked over to her truck and began to use the tire iron. She watched and was kind of put out with the ease that he loosened them. James went to loosen the final one, putting his weight and muscle into it, when the tire iron flew off the nut and the sharp end cut into his hand.

"Are you alright!?" She exclaimed.

"Yes ma'am. It looks as if you stripped this nut," James was pulling himself off the ground.

"You are saying this is my fault!" She protested looking down at him.

James got to his feet, "No, ma'am... just stating what caused the slip. I have a four socket tire tool in my truck. Let me try it."

He walked to his truck and she noticed his arm was dripping blood. She reached into her first aid kit and got him a Band-Aid.

She held out the band aid as he came back towards her, "Here ya go."

James looked down at his arm and then at her, "Oh, it is only a scratch ma'am. It will close up here directly."

"Don't be the macho cowboy. Just take it," she stated forcibly and her arm became rigid.

"Yes ma'am," he took it from her and held it up to look at it. "This is a Scooby Do Band-Aid, nice," he said smiling and then slipped it into his pocket, much to her dismay.

Susan could not believe the stubbornness of this man.

He removed the flat tire and put it in the bed of her pickup, "Do you have a spare?"

"I do, but I can take it from here.... Thanks for your help," She stuck out her hand to shake his.

James hesitated and then shook her hand, "Ummm are you sure, because it is no

21

trouble."

"I just told you I can take care of it. I'm a big girl. Thanks again," she said with a snotty tone, "so, bye now."

James thought to himself as he walked back to his truck and drove away. *"Dealing with that kind of woman was like watching the beauty of a thunderstorm roll in and getting struck by its lightening."*

As she was getting the spare that was fastened underneath the bed of her truck, she thought to herself that she might have come off a little curt to someone that was just being nice. She decided if that guy was at the Triple 7 she would apologize and thank him again.

About a mile from the homestead of the Triple 7 the white fence began on both sides of the road signaling that all of the country you could see was the ranch. James was enthusiastic about the prospect of being a foreman for such a large outfit. As he turned into the drive, the entry way boar the mark of the Triple 7; signified by three sevens together in a circle. He drove across the cattle guard and down to the main house.

The men had just finished lunch and were beginning to disperse themselves among the many pastures. Arthur Murphy was sitting on his porch, rocking in an old rocking chair letting his food settle. He was 72 years old and the ranch had been in his family for four generations. James parked and made his way to Mr. Murphy.

Mr. Murphy stood and shook his hand, "Welcome to the Triple 7, James," he said in an old gruff voice.

"Thank you, sir. I am very excited to be here," James replied enthusiastically.

"Yes, welcome indeed," a voice came from inside the screen door. Then out came the current foreman Red Lansdale. He was a husky man with dirt red hair and a long bushy mustache that might have been bright red, but was now peppered with grey.

"It is good to be here," James shook Red's hand.

Red slapped James on the shoulder, "Well, enough with the pleasantries. Let me show you around."

This kind of few words, just work, would have bothered most folks coming on to a new outfit. But how James was raised, he felt right at home.

"You'll meet most the men at supper. Let's get your things in the bunk house then we will visit the stables," Red smiled.

Red pointed towards a long narrow building on the south side of the house as they walked off the porch. James parked his truck next to the other vehicles outside the bunk house and after Red showed him his bunk he began unloading.

Susan had gotten the tire on and made her way to the ranch. She parked her truck just in front of the main house and waved to Mr. Murphy. She grabbed her gear and headed for the stables. As she walked she glanced around for the truck of the man that had helped her.

She spotted him unloading into the bunk house and thought to herself, *"Hmmm a new recruit."*

She figured she could apologize after she tended to the horses. As she entered the stables and was about to go into the first stall, she heard a voice she dreaded to hear.

"Well, hello there sweet thang," came the voice behind her.

Her skin crawled; she turned to face the distasteful presence of Little Red, Red Lansdale's only son. Little Red was big and stocky like his dad, but he was a short man which he tried to compensate for by being creepy.

"Hi, Little Red," she said short and curt. She then walked into the stable stall and closed the door behind her.

Little Red leaned against the door, "It's been awhile since we seen you around here."

"Uh, huh," she murmured as she petted the stallion in the stall.

Little Red rose up on his tip toes trying to look through the opening at the top of the stall door.

"I think you should come around and let us see you more," he whined.

Susan reached into her bag, "Just here to do my job."

"When you gonna let me take you out there, sweetness?" He patted the door.

"Go on now, Little Red, and let me work," she said without even addressing his question.

"I'll go… I'll go for a kiss…" he made a

kissing sound with his lips.

"We aren't payin her for you to try cheap come ons," a voice interrupted from the far end of the stables. Little Red looked up to see his Father and a tall cowboy standing with a horse beside him. Little Red immediately walked toward them.

"I was just teasen her, Paw," he hurried toward them.

"Mmm hmmph," Red scowled.

"This must be the foreman in training. Is that right?" Little Red reached to shake James hand. Little Red tried to crush his hand, but to his dismay it was like trying to squeeze steel.

Red looked at the flexing muscle in his son's arm and knew what he was trying to do. "That's right, and we are tending to business, I suggest you do the same."

Little Red shot an unforgiving look at his father and pushed past them both storming out of the stables. Red just shook his head.

"Sorry about that, James. That was my son. We call him Little Red and he thinks he should be the next foreman. The problem is he doesn't have the capacity for it, nor the work ethic," Red patted James on the back.

Susan had stopped what she had been doing to listen to the interaction. She heard the men begin to walk again down the fifty stall length stable. She quickly began to work on the stallion again when she heard Red call to her.

"Miss. Reddings, can you come out here and meet our future foreman?" Red knocked on the stall door.

Susan bustled about like she had been in the middle of a great many things and then opened the stall door.

"How many times do I have to tell you to call me Susan," she smiled at Red.

"Well, there is just something about your last name that I like the ring too," Red mused and they all chuckled.

James had already figured that this was going to be the woman he had helped on the road. He had spotted her truck as they left the bunk house and inquired to Red who it belonged to.

Red motioned his hand toward James, "This is James Montgomery, Miss Reddings."

"Yes sir, we have met," James tipped his hat at Susan.

"Yes, Mr. Montgomery was kind enough to help me with a flat tire," Susan smiled politely.

"Well... wonderful! Miss. Reddings might you take a look at James' horse after you are done with the other ones we called you about? We want to make sure his mount is ready to go," Red patted Blue Bonnet.

Before she could murmur a word, James

spoke, "With all due respect, I have an excellent vet back home and most things I can handle myself, but it was very nice to see you again," James smiled and shook her hand.

Susan stood there and then realized her mouth was a little open.

*"Here she was going to apologize for being a little curt and he dismisses her... who does he think he is?* She fumed.

Red sensing something was amiss, simply said, "Well, great," and ushered James to his new horse's stall about four stalls down from where Susan was standing; leaving Susan still standing there, turning a little pink in her cheeks.

She went back into her stall and let the door slam behind her. Red lifted an eyebrow as they finished in the stall and headed out the entrance of the stables.

As Susan worked she thought to

herself, "*That is exactly why I will never be with a cowboy. They are rude and have no idea how to treat a lady!*'

James smiled and shook his head as Red and he walked out of the stables, he just pictured in his mind a rattlesnake striking.

"Let's go over to my office and I will show you a few things," Red pointed to a small building on the far end of the bunk house.

"Sounds good," James nodded.

By the looks of it this must have been the original ranch house, James thought. It was a faded white house with a cracked slab porch and old block windows. As they passed through the doorway James smelled leather mixed with dust and a faint sent of mildew. There was a living room which had been turned into a waiting room and one bedroom that had been turned into the office. The kitchen still served as a kitchen, but mostly just for heating coffee nowadays. Red began to show him different office items, such as where he kept the receipts and motioned for him to sit.

Red leaned back in an old red leather office chair, "I figure, the mornings you will spend with me in here going over the books and the afternoons you spend out on the ranch so the men can come to know you and respect your work. I never ask any of the men to do a job that I haven't done." Red fixed his light blue eyes to James.

James nodded holding his hat in his hands, "Yes sir, I understand... a good policy."

Red gave a little grin and continued with his tour.

Susan finished with the horses and headed toward home. She was still irritated with roughnecks in general, but on the ride home she focused on one specific. The rude cowboy named James. When she arrived home she rushed through the door, pitched her purse on the couch and plopped down in her dad's lazy boy chair.

Her father was lying on the couch and looked up from the book he was reading, "Problem?"

Susan let out a long sigh, "Roughnecks in general, Daddy."

"Ahh, tell me what happened," he laid his book on the counter.

Susan began with the flat tire and recounted her afternoon for her Father. Pastor Reddings listened intently to his daughter's story and when she finished he kind of chuckled.

"What's so funny?" Susan said in a huff as she pressed herself into the comfort of the chair.

Her dad leaned forward on the couch as if he was about to begin interrogation, "Honey, it sounds to me that this cowboy just gave back to you what you gave to him. In my opinion, rightly so, after the way you treated someone that was helping you. What puzzles me is why he upset you so, over such a little thing. Can you tell me why you are so upset?"

"I can't explain why I am mad... I am just mad," Susan closed her eyes exhausted.

"Maybe you had better pray on it and get some rest," her dad got up to go into the kitchen, "Tomorrow will be a big day."

"What's going tomorrow?" She questioned, since it was just going to be Wednesday.

Her dad turned back from the entry way to the kitchen, "Tomorrow evening an associate pastor in training from a sister church will be assisting with the night service; I have heard good things about him," he winked.

Susan sat there for a moment mulling over this new turn of events.

Susan found herself surprisingly energized, *"The prospect of a man like daddy, how exciting*!"

She hopped up and headed for her room to pick out what she was going to wear and to talk to God about this future prospect.

Chapter Three

Learning the Ropes

James slept like a rock in his new quarters, which is really saying something with twenty two snoring cowboys in the same vicinity. The night before was fantastic. He got to meet each of the men and all of them seemed to take to him except for of course, Little Red, who made a few comments under his breath. The food was excellent; Mr. Murphy had called for some of their prime beef to be slaughtered just for his arrival.

Mr. Murphy's wife still helped in the kitchen some, but the majority of the cooking was done by Dewey Cavanal, everyone just called him Skillet. Skillet was a little thin man with a handlebar mustache and spoke with a think southern accent. James thought the outfit was lucky to have him because most of the cooks he had known, from his experience at the home ranch and hiring on with different outfits during the summer, could care less if the food tasted good to you or not. Their job was to keep you fed, plain and simple; Skillet, however, took pride in what he prepared and all the men were grateful.

After breakfast the men all went off to their work while James went with Red to the office. They talked about the beef market, what arenas to deal with and who was out to cheat you. James had been step by step with his dad in most of the ranch transactions and was very familiar with how it worked. Red was pleased with his understanding, which prompted him to overflow with information. As it neared lunch time Red showed James a map of the ranch.

He moved his finger on the map to across the road and said, "That is the North Pasture. It is divided into two 500 acre sections. We call them North Pasture East and North Pasture West. After lunch I want you to head up to the North East Pasture and help out the men who are vaccinating, castrating, and branding the new Angus calves."

"Not a problem," James nodded.

After lunch James saddled Blue Bonnet and away they went. The men had already began to work before he got there. They looked up as he rode in and then went back to their work. He took in the scene as he rode up to them. There was Jay McMullen who was roping the heads and Jose Marquez who was roping the heels. Pedro Alverez was giving the vaccinations and R.J. Reeves was doing the castrating and branding. R.J. was the newest hand to hire on six months before James. He was an average size cowboy, with a clean shaven face and always wore his hat low on his head. They had just roped their second steer as James dismounted.

He walked over to R.J. and said, "I will do the castrating," as he reached his hand out for the scalpel. All the men stopped, looked at each other for a moment and then went back to work. This was their least favorite thing to do to cattle and they all thought it was good that the future foreman was willing to do it.

It was getting close to evening time and Susan could hardly stand it, the possibility filled all her senses. They arrived early as was her Father's custom to make sure everything was in order for the service. She was sitting on the front pew trying to read her bible through a cloud of anticipation. She heard the doors at the back of the church close and watched as a man in a nice black suit walked down the center isle. He was tall, lean, and had a flowing head of black hair. Her dad walked to meet him, they shook hands and her dad motioned the young man towards her.

Her heart pounded, *"Could this be it… the moment I meet the one?"*

"Andrew Roy, this is my daughter Susan," Her dad extended his hand as if to offer her as a prize.

"It is very nice to meet you Susan," Andrew greeted her with a gentle hand shake.

She shyly smiled and looked into his eyes, "It is nice to meet you too, Andrew."

He smiled and she noticed a dimple and thought, *"This is it; he has to be the one."*

She looked him over and thought to herself, *"Yep, there is nothing cowboy about this guy."*

The evening was wonderful. She watched as Andrew earnestly helped her father with the service. After the service, to her delight, her dad invited him back to their house for ice cream. Her father and

Andrew talked awhile and then, conveniently, her mom needed her dad to help with something in the kitchen. Susan was well aware they were leaving her alone with possibly the man of her dreams. She had to be cool and calm.

"So, umm, what do you do? I mean, I know what you do; what else do you do?" She wanted to pound her head on the table. How many times did she just say "*do*?"

Andrew kind of chuckled, "Besides being an associate pastor, I work part-time at the animal shelter."

"*Ding, Ding, Ding! We have a winner! Fit me for my wedding dress right now!* She asked him a few more questions about family and his hobbies. He answered every one of them to her approval. Her parents eventually came back into the living room and Andrew thanked everyone and said goodnight. Susan sat on the couch grinning ear to ear.

Her mother smiled knowing her daughter was about to burst, "Well, he seemed like a nice boy."

"He is wonderful, smart, has a sense of humor and even works at an animal shelter!" Susan stood up, unable to contain her excitement.

"Wow," her dad looked at her mom as he sat down in his chair.

Susan was kind of pacing in a circle, "Wow is right! All the questions I asked him … he was right on with his answers."

Her mother straightened the magazines on the coffee table, "And what questions did he ask you, Honey?"

"Oh, he didn't ask me any," Susan said flippantly.

Her mother glanced at her father, "Honey, remember to not jump the gun here, you need to be patient and pray about the situation."

"Oh, I will mom, don't worry!" She hugged and kissed them goodnight and bounced into her room. Susan lay on her bed staring at the ceiling fan and contemplating her future.

"Lord, please guide me in this new relationship and help me to grow closer to the one you have for me," she whispered.

Dinner was over; it had been a long first day for James. All the hands kind of shuffled into the bunk house and prepared for bed. It smelled of old wood, leather and sweat. James really hadn't noticed it the day before, because he was too excited.

He thought to himself, it was the smell of hard work and he was pleased to be among such men.

"That was a fine meal, Skillet," one of the men said.

"I'll second that," another said.

Skillet removed his hat and bowed waving his hat below him, "Thanks yours, Thank yours."

R.J walked to the light switch, "Everybody ready?"

"Let her rip," all said.

As R.J. stood in the darkness letting his eyes adjust he noticed that James was on his knees beside his bed. R.J. had seen men pray before; you can't run around with many cowboys before you do. However, he had never seen one get on his knees to pray.

James was praying silently that he would be the man God wanted him to be and be the kind of foremen the men deserved.

Sunday came like a breath of much needed fresh air for James. The Murphy household was a Christian one and although they didn't force the men to attend church, they did enforce Sunday as the day of rest. Saturday had been very busy making sure all of the cattle and horses had what they needed for the following day. James was new to the area and figured his best bet was to go to church with the Murphy family as opposed to driving around and trying to pick a church at random. Red went along too, as James found out was his custom. Except for Red, none of the other men had ever opted to attend.

They arrived at the church about ten minutes before the service started, giving them just enough time to get their seats before the piano began to play. From the piano bench Susan was watching the clock on the back wall, waiting to begin to play on the hour, when she spotted the familiar faces of the Murphy couple and Red. But who was behind Red? She leaned in her seat.

*"Nooo it can't be him, here?"* She thought.

She was so distracted that her dad had to whisper it was time to begin. She straightened quickly and began to play.

James had noticed her as he walked in and thought to himself, *"Well I'll be, Thunderstorm can play piano."*

Then he wondered if she pounded on the keys and this brought a deep grin to his face. They sat down near the middle and James just watched her play with a slight grin on his face. It was a shame, he thought, that such a beautiful woman would have such a foul disposition.

They finished the first hymn and the Pastor got up to give the announcements. Susan's eyes glanced over to James; he was watching her father intently. She finished the next couple of hymns, sat next to her mother on the front row and determined not to give James another thought. Despite her effort, she wasn't listening to the sermon; her father's words were reverberating in her brain, *"What puzzles me is why he upset you so, over such a little thing. Can you tell me why you are so upset?"* She was utterly convicted and felt she owed James a sincere apology.

*"He had just tried to help her and he was*

*met with hostility,"* she thought, *"I will set this right."*

After all she needed to be ready with a clean conscience if her new relationship with Andrew blossomed.

After church Susan made a bee line for James. He was busy shaking hands and talking with the people Red and the Murphy couple had introduced to him.

*"I am waiting ever so patiently,"* Susan thought.

He had noticed her walk up and figured by their first encounter she would just interrupt, but she didn't. James pulled away from the conversation and turned to her.

"Good Mornin', Miss. Reddings," James shook her hand. His grip was solid as an oak tree but he didn't hurt her.

Susan ran her hair behind her ear on the left side, "Good morning, Mr. Montgomery. I...," she hesitated.

James cut in, "I didn't figure on seeing you here."

Susan was taken aback, "What do you mean; you didn't figure on seeing me here?"

James smiled at her and thought to himself, *"This girl would pick a fight with a tree stump."*

"Nothing ma'am, it was just a surprise is all," he said evenly.

She was dazed, "A… a surprise?"

Did he mean she wasn't the kind of person he thought would be at church because of how she treated him or could it be as simple as he just didn't know that she would be there?

"Well, we are heading out; it was nice to see ya again," he said as he walked to the back of the church holding his hat in his hand.

Susan stood frozen again becoming self

aware that her mouth had come open slightly. She abruptly shut it and sat down in the pew. She got mad all over again.

*"He continues to make saying sorry so difficult,* she thought. *What kind of person does he think I am and why do I even care?"*

She decided right then and there in that pew that she wasn't going to dwell on this nonsense. When she saw James again she would apologize before he could utter a word.

*"That will be that!"* She thought, *"and then I can focus on more pressing matters, like Andrew coming to the next Wednesday night service."*

On the ride back to the ranch, Mr. Murphy had opted for Red to drive them back. This decision was favorable to the rest of the passengers since Mr. Murphy drove like he was herding cats.

Mr. Murphy turned in his seat to look back at James, "I saw you talking to the Reddings girl."

"Yes sir," James nodded, not giving up any information.

Mr. Murphy smiled at James and turned back in his seat. He looked at Red, "Hmmph, a fine family the Reddings, Good people, wouldn't you say Red?"

"They don't come better," Red stated never moving an eye from the road.

"Humph, yep, good people," Mr. Murphy reiterated and slapped his knee.

James thought to himself, "*Not from what I have seen, but maybe the daughter is just the black sheep. What is this conversation about? Get James hitched? I have more pressing matters, like becoming a foreman and eventually owning my own ranch.*"

## Chapter 4

*El Gato*

Slim Golding and Jose Marquez rode in hard and fast on Monday morning. James and Red were in the process of going through the cattle breeds and the lineages of their prize cattle. When Slim and Jose bust through the door, both men looked up at them. Red knew immediately that something was wrong.

Red stood up, "What's happened?!"

"We found one calf dead and one more is missing," Slim said in a deep voice.

Jose made a scratching movement with his hand, "El Gato, señor. We found his tracks."

Red looked at the two men, "Are you sure? Mountain lions aren't supposed to be in these parts anymore."

"There is no mistaking it. The track was too big for a bobcat," Slim put his hands about seven inches apart, "And we found a blood trail where it dragged the calf."

Red sat back in his chair and rubbed his hands over his face, "How do you think we should handle this, James?"

James said a silent prayer for God to give him wisdom in this.

"Well... the cat obviously is eating in the same area. We could bait him and kill him."

"Good, good... They hunt at dawn and dusk mostly though," Red ran his fingers down his long mustache.

James looked at each man as he spoke, "We should send a group of men to camp about two hundred yards from where we'll put the raw meat. They can take shifts watching for the cat at a safe shooting distance."

"Excellent idea, James," Red smiled and slapped the arms of his chair.

James pointed up, "I just asked God for wisdom, is all."

Red winked at him and when all the men came in for lunch they discussed the particulars. Red had determined that James was to lead the outing with four other men, Jose, R.J, Slim, and Little Red. They packed their bed rolls and a few camping supplies, and then rode out about two hours before Sundown. Slim and Jose directed James to where the dead calf had been and where the blood trail started. They found a small mesquite tree just between the two areas and James said this will be perfect for a clear shot. He hung about five pounds of raw meat in the tree and pointed to a large rock about seventy five yards away.

"That is where we will shoot from."

They made camp. James took first watch.

He walked down to the hiding place and leaned over the rock with the 3'06 Red had loaned the men to use. The men didn't carry guns unless they were having coyote or wild dog problems, and it had been so long since that had occurred there was only Red's rifle and Mr. Murphy's shotgun left on the ranch. The rest of the guns had left the ranch as the men who owned them moved on or sold them at the pawn shop. Red's rifle was bolt action with a Bushnell scope and James focused it to perfection on the mesquite tree. He was fortunate that the moon was set to be big and bright for the next couple of days. He waited with anticipation, but no mountain lion came.

Slim walked down to relieve James a little past midnight. The men figured just because a mountain lion usually hunted at dusk and dawn didn't mean it wouldn't hunt at night.

James turned to look at the sound of

footsteps coming, "Are the other men asleep?"

Slim shook his head, "Nope, playing cards. You see anything?"

James handed Slim the gun, "Not even a coyote."

James walked back to the camp and enjoyed the cool midnight breeze; it was peaceful here with the sound of the cicadas talking to each other. His peaceful moment was interrupted as he reached the camp site. He saw Little Red on top of Jose choking him.

"I know you cheated me, you dirty Mexican!" Little Red squeezed Jose's throat.

R.J. was trying to calm Little Red down but to no avail.

"Let him loose!" James said in a deep echoing voice.

Everyone looked at James.

"He cheated me and he is going to pay!"

Little Red yelled and continued choking Jose.

"Let him loose!" James replied like an old hound dog barking at a treed coon.

Little Red spit in James' direction, "What if I don't, foreman in training?"

James took four steps towards him, "Then you and I will have a serious disagreement, right here and right now."

Little Red released Jose and got up, "Alright, alright... See I let him loose," pointing to Jose.

"Head back to the bunk house, Little Red," James pointed toward the homestead.

Little Red kicked the dirt and picked up his hat, "You're not the foreman yet! You don't have the right to tell me to go."

"I am the lead on this outing and you will either go of your own accord or I'll drag you there," James stated in such a way that there was no room for question.

Little Red kicked over the table sending the cards and chips into the dirt, "Fine, I didn't want to sleep on the ground anyways!"

Little Red saddled his horse and rode away. Jose was sitting up still holding his throat; James knelt down next to him.

James took a hold of his forearm, "Are you alright?"

"Sí, señor... I no cheat him," Jose managed in his broken English.

"I didn't figure you did," James said assuredly and helped Jose to his feet.

James put his hand on R.J.'s shoulder since he was still standing there in awe of such an intense scene.

"Let's all get some sleep and get that cat," James turned the table back on its legs.

The night continued without a sign of the

mountain lion. Dawn came quickly and all the men were a little stiff from sleeping on the ground. James packed the raw meat back up and they headed back to the homestead to start their daily jobs. They missed breakfast, but Skillet saved them enough to fill their bellies for which they were eternally grateful.

Skillet slapped the food on their plates, "Did your see' um?"

"Not a sign of him all night," James replied and then bowed his head to say a quick silent prayer of thanks.

Skillet didn't notice James' head bowed because he was lost in thought.

Skillet's thoughts spilled over into words, "Hmmm, ya know back when I was with the Lazy T ranch in El Paso, we had er a coyote problem. We tried that raw meat, but them ol coyotes wouldn't come near. So we soaked that meat in some cattle blood and sure is shootin they came runnin like their tales were on fire."

James had managed to hear what Skillet was saying during his prayer, "That is a great idea, do you think you can do that for us before we go out tonight."

"Will do'er," Skillet rubbed his hands together.

After Jose and R.J finished their breakfast they went on to their designated pastures. James went to the office where he found Red sorting cattle breeding information. James came in and sat down without a word. He was not pleased with Red's son and he didn't want to reflect that in his voice.

Red watched James as he came in and sat down, "Mornin' James, did you get it?"

"Mornin' Red, no sir we didn't see him," James shook his head.

Red made a deep sigh, "I saw my boy was

at breakfast…must have had a problem with him."

"Yes, sir… but I handled it. He won't be going back out with us tonight," James said in a way that closed the door on that topic.

Red smiled, "Alright then."

He grew more and more impressed with James' character. Most men would have complained or whined about an issue; James was not that kind of man.

Before evening came the three men rode out to the camp sight. James hung the soaked meat on the mesquite tree and R.J. took first watch. It was just after sundown when all the men started hearing the coyotes howl.

James laid in his sleeping bag thinking, *"Great, now we will have coyotes all over us and no mountain lion."*

R.J.'s senses were on end. He could hear the howling getting closer and sure enough three coyotes started jumping at the meat trying to get up the mesquite tree. R.J. was uncertain what to do. They didn't care for coyotes either. He considered starting to shoot them. R.J. was focusing on them through his scope when a flash of light brown filled his scope view. He looked over the rock with his naked eye and saw the mountain lion swatting at the coyotes. Knowing he only had moments before the big cat would grab the meat and be gone, R.J. grabbed the gun, adjusted the scope sites right on the cat and squeezed the trigger. The sound of the report of the rifle awoke Jose and James and they came running. R.J. was standing behind the rock waiting for them.

"I hit him, but I didn't kill him...He went that way into that think brush," R.J. pointed at a nearby thicket of Mesquite trees and underbrush.

James looked at both of the men, "We need to finish him. A wounded cat can be more dangerous."

All three men took their flashlights out and found the blood trail.

James looked down at the blood trail, "Ok if you spot him, holler and R.J. you be read with that gun."

The men followed the trail into the brush just where R.J. had pointed. They had walked about twenty yards into the brush and lost the blood trail. The three men split up slowing walking in different directions.

James came to a small ravine surrounded by mesquite trees. He turned to make sure he could still see the yellow glow of the men's flashlights moving back and forth as they searched. He had taken two steps down the slop into the ravine, when he heard the big cat breathing. It was so close to him. James froze where he was; the breathing was heavy and quickly paced. He slowly moved the flashlight looking at the ground and the underbrush, when a terrifying realization came over him that the cat had gotten behind him. He started to slowly turn around when the cat jumped onto him from the base of a mesquite tree.

The force at which the cat hit him knocked him head first down into the ravine. His flashlight flew into the air and busted on a nearby rock. His head and shoulder had scrapped over the rock bed and he could feel himself bleeding, his face covered with mud and blood. He managed to role over only to find the cat lunging toward him. James raised his arms to cover his head and the cat bit deep into his left forearm. The pain was excruciating, as he tried to move the cat back from his face with his punctured arm. James remembered his knife on his belt; he grabbed it and just as the cat was releasing his arm to bite him again.

James cut its throat and kicked it off of him.

He was bleeding badly from his arm and head, but somehow he managed to stand up and yell for his companions. He managed to walk out of the ravine, when he started to see black spots appearing and he fell to one knee. The last thing he saw before he blacked out was Jose's flashlight running to him.

Chapter 5

The Perky Nurse


Wednesday night service had finally come. Susan had been anticipating this day since last Wednesday. Andrew showed up early again to her complete enjoyment. He was dressed in a dark blue suit and she thought if it was possible he looked even more handsome than the Wednesday before. She played the worship introduction as everyone came in and then her dad stood up for announcements.

"I want to remind everyone that our youth group is washing cars this Saturday to raise money for their mission trip to Mexico. So bring them dirty. The youth are ready, willing, and able. We need to continue to pray for Mary Putnam, as most of you know she fell last Friday and busted her hip."

Susan was halfway listening; she was just

looking at how confidently Andrew was sitting in the front row watching her father.

"We also need to be in prayer for the new hand on the Triple 7 ranch, James Montgomery was attacked by a mountain lion and he lost a lot of blood."

Susan thought, *"Wait... what did he just say? James... Attacked!"*

Her dad was now looking at her, since she missed her queue to start playing Amazing Grace. As she began to play her head was spinning.

*"How in the world did a mountain lion attack him,"* she thought, *"There weren't mountain lions in these parts anymore."*

She needed more details and she was going to have to wait until after the service. The service took its normal time, but she felt like it lasted forever. Finally, the church members were dismissed and she began to go directly to her father but standing in her way was Andrew. She looked up at him from her seat at the piano.

Andrew had his hands deep in his pockets, "So Susan, I was wondering what you were doing Friday night?"

Susan blushed, "Oh, I umm I have nothing going on," forgetting all about James.

"Well, I was wondering if you might want to go to dinner and a movie," Andrew smiled showing off his dimple.

*Andrew looked positively pristine in his dark suit and gold tie,* she thought. "I would love that!" She said a little too loudly.

Andrew ran his hand back and forth on the piano top, "Alright, cool... Pick you up at six?"

"That will work," she said beaming.

On that note Andrew turned, said goodnight to her dad and walked out of the sanctuary. Susan sat on the piano bench and watched him all the way out. Her dad's voice brought her out of la la land.

"You ready to go, Susan?" Her dad inquired as he walked up to her.

Susan blinked her eyes a little unnerved, "Oh... yes I am ready."

As they were walking out she remembered James, "Dad, so what happened to the new hand at the Triple 7?"

Her dad opened the door for her to walk out, "Apparently, from what Mr. Murphy told me, that tough cowboy took on a mountain lion that was killing the cattle, hand to hand and he killed it with a knife."

"How bad is he hurt?" She passed by him and down the steps.

Her dad followed, unlocking the car door with his remote, "Pretty bad from what Mr. Murphy said, the mountain lion apparently bit into an artery vain and James lost a lot of blood before they could get him to the hospital. I am going to head out to the hospital tomorrow morning to see him."

"Well... Uh, if you wait until lunch time I will go with you," Susan said before she got into the car.

"Oh yeah?" Her dad raised an eyebrow as he buckled his seatbelt.

She nodded, "He was the one who helped me with the flat tire. It's the least I could do," seeming a little put out as she buckled her belt. She thought, *Well at least now if he is ok I can apologize and he can't walk away.*"

Her dad started out of the parking lot, "Oh... I see." He smiled and left it at that.

James awoke to a nurse checking his I.V. before her shift ended, on Thursday morning. He looked around his hospital room as his eyes cleared. His parents were there, both trying to sleep in uncomfortable chairs.

James leaned up from his bed, "Now, you would think they would at least give you two army cots or something." James voice was as clear and solid as it ever was.

Both of his parents woke to the sound of his voice and rushed to him.

James took each of their hands, "How long have I been out?"

"Bout twenty four hours, son," his dad grinned.

James could tell both his parents were filled with emotion. It must have really scared them.

His mom kissed his forehead, "How are you feeling?"

"Aww I suppose, I will be ready to fight another one in a day or so," James mused.

Both his parents smiled. They knew if he was making jokes he was alright.

"You lost a lot of blood, son," his dad

cautioned.

James gripped his father's hand, "Yeah, but you should see the cat."

They all chuckled.

"I suppose someone from the ranch called you?" James raised his eyebrows.

His mom nodded, "Yes, Mr. Murphy called us straight away."

"They are sure good people," James affirmed.

The day nurse came in to check on him. She had blond hair with a pixy style to it, crystal blue eyes and might have weighed a buck fifteen soaking wet. She came striding towards him.

"Oh! You're awake! That is wonderful!" She exclaimed in a perky voice, "How is the pain?" She laid her note board on James' legs and took hold of his bed rail with both hands.

James looked over and read her name

tag, "Well, Tina, pain reminds me it is there," he smiled.

She giggled, "Alright then we will give you something for the pain. Are you feeling sick at your stomach or light headed?" She kind of turned her head from side to side as if she was bouncing a thought back and forth in her head.

James gave her the O.K. sign with his fingers, "No ma'am I am good."

She smiled as she picked up the board and wrote something down on it, "Great! I will be back in bit with some pain medication and maybe some food?"

"Sounds great, thanks Tina," he smirked.

"Anytime, cowboy," she said as she practically bounced out the door.

James glanced at his father, who just winked at him. His mother grinned and sat back in her chair.

His dad and he talked about the mountain lion fight and the entire goings on at the ranches throughout the remainder of the morning.

"Where did good ol Tina go? My belly button is rubbing a blister on my backbone," James rubbed his stomach in a circular motion.

About that time there came a knock on the door.

"Come on in," James called.

He watched as the Preacher from the church he visited came through the door and low and behold behind him was the Storm! He figured if she starting something in here, his mom would take her. James leaned up and shook Pastor Reddings' hand.

James motioned to his parents, "Mom and Dad, this is Pastor Reddings and his daughter."

"*And his Daughter!*" Susan thought, as both her and her dad shook hands with his parents.

The little hospital room suddenly became

very small and James' dad was feeling a bit claustrophobic.

"Well... we are going to run and get something to eat and let ya'll visit," Mr. Montgomery moved towards the door nodding at the Pastor and his daughter.

James' mom had been married to the man some 30 years and she knew him well enough just to follow his lead. She kissed her son on the head again and out the door they went.

"I sure appreciate ya'll taking the time to come and see me, with me not being a member of your church and all," James rose up his bed to sit more upright.

Pastor Reddings pulled a chair over to James' bed, "From what I hear we are family in Christ, membership has nothing to do with it. So how are you feeling?"

"Aww kind of like I wrestled a Mountain

Lion," James smirked.

"I guess that's about right," Pastor Reddings laughed.

Susan hadn't said a word. She was just standing and watching her dad with James. She was going over her apology in her head. When out of the blue the attention was unexpectedly put on her.

James pointed at her and smiled, "That daughter you have there is quite independent, wouldn't even let me finish changing her flat tire."

Her dad looked at her. "Yes, indeed... she can have a strong mind sometimes," Pastor Reddings grinned.

"Well... I am glad you brought that up..." Susan stepped closer, "I have been meaning to..."

The hospital door flung open, "Alright! I have some soothing drugs and some hearty food for the cowboy!" A perky voice announced.

They all turned to see a bouncing nurse

coming right a James.

"Hey Tina! James grinned. "Where have ya been? I'm starving," he then motioned with his hands like he was put out.

"Oh Hun, I had to make a special trip to get you something decent to eat," Tina beamed as she carried his food and medication.

*"Hun...special trip... who is this lady?,"* Susan thought.

Tina stepped in front of the Reddings and went to tending to James. She hooked another bag to his IV, laid some food out for him and then began to take his pulse with her hand on his wrist. Susan watched this and seemed to be the only one that picked up on the fact that he was already on a heart monitor.

*"This lady just wanted to touch him,"* Susan was flabbergasted.

"Sorry, to interrupt, alright cowboy, if you

need anything you just push that little button right there and I will come running," Tina padded James on the arm.

*"I just bet you will,"* Susan thought.

Tina bounced out of the room, leaving the three of them alone again.

Pastor Reddings looked over James' food, "That looks good for hospital food."

James opened the container, "I am not sure it is hospital food," he winked at Pastor Reddings.

Susan stood rigid, "AS I WAS SAYING," she said rather loudly.

Both men looked at her like she just ripped a phone book in half.

She straightened, "About the tire changing, I wanted to say I was sorry for being so curt with you and to thank you again for your help." There she had said it, it was done.

"You mean you're not that way all the

time?" James grinned and her dad laughed.

Her eyes went wide, "No, I am not that way all the time..."

James smiled at her, "Aww well... Think nothing of it Miss. Reddings; I was just glad I could help a little bit."

"So James, what are you doing for the Murphys at the ranch?" Pastor Reddings asked.

"I am training to be their next foreman," James lifted up his bandaged arm to suggest that was part of his training and smiled.

"Oh wow, so not just another hand then," Pastor Reddings stated with approval.

"Well, sir, a good foreman is another hand and many times he needs to be the first hand in the work and the last hand out. I believe in Colossians it says... *In all the work you are doing, work the best you can. Work as if you were doing it for the Lord, not for people.* I try to live by that," James explained.

"Well said," Pastor Reddings smiled.

Susan was surprised, a cowboy that can quote scripture. She didn't see that coming.

James must have seen the surprise on her face because he called her on it. "You look surprised, Miss Reddings. You didn't think rough necks could ride with the Lord?"

"Well, I umm..." She began to blush.

"That is exactly what she thought," her dad nodded.

Susan looked at her father with an embarrassed, 'we are going to discuss this later' look.

"Oh that's alright. I was beginning to think all veterinarians were like thunderstorms," James chuckled and so did her dad.

Susan couldn't help the grin that came across her face.

Pastor Reddings stood up and shook James' hand, "Ok, well, we are going to get out of here and let you rest. Is there anything you need?"

James warmed as he shook the pastor's hand, "Other than prayer for quick healing, I am good sir. Thank you both for coming to see me."

They both said bye and after her dad had passed the doorway, James called to Susan, "Oh, and Miss Reddings, you did strip that nut."

Susan spun on her heals with a grin on her face.

"A thunderstorm... huh, then you better watch out for my lightning strike," she kidded.

"Yes, for the lightening and something else," James nodded and grinned.

"What else?" She looked puzzled.

"Maybe one day I'll tell you. See you Sunday if I am out of here, Miss Reddings," James smiled.

"Call me Susan," she said and was gone.

James laid his head back deep into the

pillow and looked up at the white ceiling. *"She wasn't that bad after all. A little high strung but that made joking with her all the more fun."*

He thought back to the few girls he had dated growing up. How every one of them only wanted the cowboy and not the Christian. When he would talk to them about walking with the Lord or want to talk about the bible, their eyes would just glaze over. *"I guess even pastor's daughters think a cowboy is just a cowboy."*

As Susan and her dad walked to the car, he could tell she was in deep thought.

"That was a nice visit. He seems like a good guy," her dad said as he looked both ways at the intersection.

"Yes, it was," Susan was following a step behind her dad crossing the road, an unconscious training from when she was holding his hand as a child.

"He appears to know the Lord," her dad unlocked the car doors.

"Yes, it appears he does," Susan hopped into the car, not waiting for more conversation.

Her dad slid into the driver's seat right after her, "And he is a cowboy..."

Susan turned and faced her dad, knowing when he got a hold of something it was best to discuss it because he wasn't going to let it go.

"I know where you are going with this dad. Yes... I get it ... I should not have judged the man just because he is a cowboy. However, just because he knows the Lord does not mean he knows how to treat a lady. I believe that was my point before," she said as she snapped her seatbelt.

Her dad raised his eye brows, "Well, that's true. It doesn't mean he knows how to treat a lady, but it doesn't mean he doesn't know either."

"I got it, Dad... I don't need to judge people

before I know them," Susan patted his hand, making sure he understood she was listening.

As they drove away it began to rain. She watched the drops hit the windshield and the windshield wiper blades move over them. They didn't speak as her dad drove her back to her office. Her dad figured she had some sorting out to do. Susan thought about her previous relationships with cowboys or farm hands. Everyone she had ever went on a date with, treated her like she was just a regular girl and it was just a another date. Not one of them had taken her breath away, or even impressed her in the slightest with romance.

She glanced over at her father. It is his entire fault; she grew up watching her dad dazzle her mom. It was the little things he did, how he would remember her mom's favorite things and somehow come up with them. He would remember things that even she forgot she'd said she liked and always seem to just overwhelm her with them. How could those guys even come close to that? She thought the closest she ever came was when one cowboy brought her flowers; except she could see the price tag and that he had just picked them up at the gas station. "*A lot of thought was put into that*," she remembered thinking.

It was great that Mr. Montgomery was a Christian, but the odds on him being a man like her dad were not good. He probably wasn't interested in her anyways, which wasn't an issue because she had a date with Andrew Friday. She had no doubt he was cookie cutter her dad. After all he was an associate pastor and loved animals.

Chapter 6

Just Like Dad


Friday night, date night... She had thought about this date all day long. She had a beautiful sun dress to wear and had indulged herself by leaving work early to get her nails done, which she was sure Andrew would notice. She wanted to make sure she was 100 percent ready when he arrived. She was ready to go fifteen minutes early which was a terrible thing, because now she had to wait. She wasn't that good at waiting. She was excellent at pacing and so she began.

Her dad came in from mowing the grass, saw his daughter, and asked "Is he late?"

"No," she paced.

Her dad looked at the clock on the wall, "When do you expect him?"

"In about 5 minutes," she never slowed her pace.

Her dad watched her for a moment going back and forth, "Alright, I hope he is on time or I am going to need to get a new rug," he chuckled.

"Ha, ha... Very funny," Susan smiled.

Her dad always had a way of teasing her that made her feel better.

The reflection of light bounced off the front window. Andrew had arrived a little early.

Susan rushed to her room, "Dad can you get the door?!" She yelled as she flew by him.

"Of course, Honey," he grinned.

Andrew knocked on the door and her father opened it. She could hear polite conversation and then her dad called for her as she knew he would.

"Susan, your date is here!" He turned and called down the hall.

"Be right there!" Susan called back.

She waited two minutes and walked out. Andrew looked great in his khaki Dockers and green golf shirt. It was as if he had just been golfing with the Kennedys.

Andrew smiled as he looked at her, "Are you ready?"

"I am now," Susan blushed.

"You two have fun," her dad said as they walked out the door.

Susan remembered that her dad's farewell used to include the time for the boy to have her home. After she turned twenty one, he finally decided she was grown enough to decide that for herself. She never stayed out past midnight anyway, so he was good with that.

Andrew and Susan walked to his car; he got into the driver's seat. She paused for a moment, then walked around and got in.

"Are you hungry?" Andrew started the car.

Susan was busy getting on her seatbelt, "Famished."

"Good deal. How does Chinese sound?" Andrew asked, clicking off his radio that came on with the start of his car.

"Fine with me, I like Chinese," she smiled.

"Awesome," Andrew put the car in gear and they were off.

They were seated with no wait at the restaurant. Susan had come to Cho Wang's restaurant since she was a kid. She loved it because it had dim lighting and cushy booths to sit in. They ordered drinks and looked through their menus.

"So what do you do for a living?" Andrew inquired never looking up from his menu.

Susan looked at him, "I am a Veterinarian."

"Oh yeah, that's cool." Andrew turned another page of the menu.

Silence hit the table as they continued to

look at their menus.

After what seemed like forever, Susan broke the silence, "I just love animals."

"Makes sense," Andrew nodded and put his menu down.

The waitress came and took their orders and then disappeared to the back. Andrew was now looking at her and she just beamed with this prospect.

Susan stirred her ice tea with her spoon, "So have you always wanted to be a pastor?"

"No, not always, I heard the call when I was in college. A friend of mine had died in a drunk driving accident when I realized that I had never shared Christ with him. The Lord began to convict me about the major in biology I was seeking and drew me into the ministry." Andrew squeezed lemon into his water.

"Wow, life changing. What school did you go to?" Susan tasted her tea.

"A & M," Andrew said.

"So you're an Aggie?" Susan smiled.

"Yes, I am... And no Aggie jokes allowed," Andrew pointed his finger at Susan.

"Will do," Susan blushed.

The evening continued on like that with conversation between awkward silences, which Susan was used to on most of her first dates. The movie Andrew had picked was a romantic comedy, which was a breath of fresh air to Susan. It seemed she always ended up going to action movies with other dates.

*"Andrew is great,"* she thought, *"He had strong convictions about God, he has paid for the date, picked a movie that he thought I would like and even offered to get me popcorn."*

They arrived back at Susan's home about 10:30 P.M. Dad had left the porch light on for her. Andrew got out and walked her to her door. They stopped at the doorway and looked at each other.

"I had a great time," Andrew said.

"So did I," Susan held her hands together and looked up at him.

Andrew ran his fingers through his hair, "Are you up for doing it again, next Friday?"

"That would be great!" Susan beamed.

They gave each other a quick little hug and Andrew was gone.

Susan was on air as she floated to her room. "He is it, the more I get to know him the more I like him." She mused.

She couldn't wait until their next date! She got on her knees and thanked God for such a great time. Then she hopped into bed and replayed the entire date in her head.

Chapter 7

To The Rescue

Sunday morning rolled around and Susan
was at her usual church service perch preparing to
play the piano. She wondered if Mr. Montgomery
would be able to make it today. About ten minutes
before the service started, in came the Murphys, Red,
and sure enough a bandaged Mr. Montgomery. She
was glad to see that he was alright and prided herself
on apologizing to him.

After the service she was putting the hymn
music under the seat, when she heard a deep West
Texas accent say "Susan..." She looked up from the
bench and saw James standing there.

He was as big as life, holding his black
Stetson in his hands and smiling that smile of his. "I
just wanted to thank you again for coming to see

me."

"Of course, Mr. Montgomery, it was our pleasure," Susan straightened the hymn music on the piano.

James looked down at her hands, "I see you got your nails done. They look nice."

"Aww, thank you," Susan smiled. Then she realized that Andrew hadn't noticed. Her face suddenly became solemn in thought.

"James! How are you feeling?" Pastor Reddings interrupted.

"Doing great, sir, thanks again for the prayers," James turned and shook his hand.

"Of course," Pastor Reddings smiled.

James began to back away as he spoke, "Well, I better catch my ride before they leave without me."

"See ya," Susan gave a little wave.

"Bye James," her dad echoed.

James looked forward to getting back to work with the men. When he came home on Saturday, Red gave him strict instructions that until he was healed up he would be spending all day in the office with Red learning the paper work. Most of the men greeted him as if he had defeated Goliath. Apparently Jose was quite the story teller when you got him going.

The next week was long and hard for the men. They had to take all the first year steers to market and it was pouring rain all week. James wanted to help them, but Red insisted he stay put.

The Ranch did really well at the market and to show his appreciation, Mr. Murphy gave each of the men a money bonus. This included James, despite his protest. So on Friday night most of the men headed for town to celebrate.

Andrew continued to please Susan. He

showed up early again, asked where she wanted to eat, picked another romantic comedy and again bought her popcorn. She joked with him about doing the same thing again and he assured her that the next time they would do something different.

They had just finished another great movie and were walking to his car when she heard that voice she dreaded.

"Wooo, Miss. Vet. is on the town!" Little Red slurred as he crossed the street toward them.

Susan laced Andrew's arm and started to walk faster towards the car.

Little Red noticed this and picked up his speed behind them, "Hey, Hey... where ya in a rush to?"

Andrew turned to look, "Do you know that guy?"

"Unfortunately, he can be a creep. We need to get in the car," Susan advised and picked up walking speed.

They hurried to the car. It was backed into the parking space with a building at its rear and a car on either side. Andrew and Susan jumped in, and buckled up. They were about to drive away, when in front of the car stood Little Red, blocking their escape. He had his hat tipped back on his head and was holding a beer bottle in his right hand. His eyebrows pointed down into a frown, which gave them notice that he was not pleased that they were trying to leave.

"You think you are too good to talk to me!" Little Red kicked at the car missing it and nearly falling down.

"Who is that with you, your little date? How come you can go out with this bean pole and not me, HUH?" Little Red screamed again.

This time he threw his beer bottle at the car bouncing it off the hood and shattering it on the pavement.

Andrew rolled down the window a little bit, "Look mister, we don't want any trouble."

Susan looked at Andrew. He had turned pale and was slowing putting the car into gear. Susan looked back at Little Red who had started making his way toward the driver's door.

"You don't want trouble, huh?" Little Red stumbled toward them, "I'll show you what a real man can do."

"Drive Around him!" She yelled at Andrew.

Before Andrew could press on the gas, Little Red already had opened Andrew's door and was reaching over the top of it to get him. Andrew was buckled in and had nowhere to go. Just as Little Red was about to grab a hold of Andrew's collar, all of a sudden, he fell to his knees and hit his head on the window of the car door. Standing on the back of one of Little Red's knees was a bandaged James

Montgomery.

"I think ya aught leave these nice people in peace," James was sternly looking down at Little Red.

Little Red reached for his hat that had popped off when he banged his head, "We ain't on the ranch and you better be careful with that bandaged arm!"

"You may be right, but my feet still work," James dug his boot heel into the back of Little Red's knee.

"Now you can go on your way or I'm going to put these boots to walking up your body, your choice." James continued just as calm as if he was on a Sunday drive.

Little Red tried to move a little bit but James just dug in that boot heel, "Alright... Alright I'll go!"

James lifted his leg watching him closely.

Little Red scampered forward, "This isn't over, Trainee!" He pushed the door shut and squeezed behind the other car and the wall and left through the parking lot.

"I didn't figure it was," James sighed to himself.

James peered down into the car and saw both Andrew and Susan wide eyed and a little pale.

"Ya'll all right?" James smiled.

Andrew drew a long breath and then smiled back and nodded.

Susan got out of the car, "We're ok, thank you so much."

"Not a thang, ya'll have a nice night," James tipped his hat to Susan and went walking down the side walk.

Susan got back in the car and Andrew without a word pulled out of the parking lot. As they started down the road, Susan saw James walking to his truck. There was someone waiting by it.

"Is *that? Surely NOT! Nooo the perky nurse!*" Susan was astonished. She watched as James opened up his truck door on the passenger side and Miss. Perky hopped in. *"How he could go for a girl like that,"* she thought.

"Well, I hope our next date is less eventful," Andrew laughed nervously.

"Me too," Susan replied, but her mind was on James.

Andrew drove her home, walked her to the door and gave her a quick hug goodnight. She went inside, laid her purse on the counter and went to her room. As she knelt next to her bed to pray, she found she didn't know what to pray. The script like prayer about finding *the one* just didn't come out. She began to pray for Little Red instead and thanked the Lord that James came along when he did. She crawled into bed, closed her eyes and tried to sleep.

Two hours passed, she threw the covers off of her and clicked on the lamp next to her bed.

"It is useless!" She said in a huff to herself.

There were too many things going on in her mind and they were not about to shut off. She sat on her bed and thought, "*O.K., I just need to process all that happened tonight and then I will be able to sleep.*"

She began with the date, which she thought was wonderful. The encounter with Little Red which was still scary, and then James coming to the rescue, again...

She thought, "*With a bandaged arm no less.*"

Then she remembered seeing Miss. Perky getting into James' truck. "*He opened her door.... STOP IT,*" she thought to herself as she slapped the bed. *"Everything is going great with Andrew. James obviously has a different taste in women. You don't need to get mixed up now."*

She determined in her mind that she would focus on God's guidance with Andrew and laid her head on her pillow. Susan began to drift off to sleep and the thought, *"James opened her door,"* whispered in her mind.

Chapter 8

The Stampede

Saturday morning came too early after a date night as Saturday mornings seems to do. After breakfast James went in for his usual office work with Red. This morning something was different. Red seemed troubled.

"How are ya this morning?" James inquired sensing something wrong.

"Sit down, James," Red motioned to a chair.

James sat in the old wicker chair next to the office desk, "What's up, Red?"

"Well... Slim came to talk to me this morning before breakfast. It seems you and Little Red had a run in last night?" Red looked to his boots.

"Yes, sir," James nodded.

"Well... the way Slim says it is that Little

Red said you embarrassed him and he went on all last night about how he's gonna pay you back," Red said as he looked at James.

"I know Little Red was drunk and I have no doubt whatever happened you were justified in it. However, you need to be on your toes, because my son doesn't forget..." Red trailed off.

"Understood," James said in such a way that nothing more needed to be discussed.

The next week went by quickly. James was healing up nicely and was allowed to go out and work cattle with the men. He hadn't had any trouble with Little Red, they just kind of steered clear of each other.

Pedro's horse got rattlesnake bit on Saturday morning and they called the vet out to take a look at it. Red had mentioned to James that Susan was coming out and gave him a wink. James just smiled at him.

James thought, "*I am glad everyone is so worried about my love life, especially with someone who seems to be doing fine dating someone else.*"

As the week had gone by, Susan had talked to Andrew on the phone a few times and had a date with him for tonight. So she wasn't pleased when the call came in to go out to the Triple 7 for a horse with snakebite. She was instantly nervous and then extremely mad because she was nervous. She took a quick look in the mirror before heading out to the ranch. When she arrived, she found herself looking around for James despite her resolution not to. She was thankful that Red and Pedro met her at the stables, because that meant no Little Red issues. They assisted her as she got to work on the poisoned horse.

Around that same time in the South East pasture James and some other men were corralling their Long Horn herd. They had been having a really bad time with flies this season and they all needed dusting. James herded the last few into the coral and R.J. shut the gate. Little Red, Slim, and R.J. were assigned to dust them; James was excluded to prevent infection to his arm.

While the men were working, James walked Blue Bonnet down to a nearby stream to let her drink. He leaned down over the saddle and rubbed her neck. All of a sudden there was a gunshot, and then came the sound of thunder heading their way. James knew the sound of a stampede. James took the reins and kicked his heels quickly into his horse. Blue Bonnet jumped through the stream. The embankment on the other side was steep and filled with large rocks.

The cattle were already rushing through the water, when Blue Bonnet's back foot slipped on a rolling rock. She screamed in pain as one of the bulls speared her back left leg. Her eyes went wide as she started to turn broadside sliding down the embankment. A cow hit her under the chest and she buckled. James knew she was about to roll, he leaped off onto the rocks as she rolled once into a large bolder.

James hit the rocks hard. He knew as the pain shot up his left side the he had busted up his leg. He watched in horror as another bull speared Blue Bonnet in the side. James was rolling the best he could to avoid the pounding hooves of the cattle as they all rushed up the embankment. Then there was only the sound of Blue Bonnet screaming is the haze of dust and pain.

Blood was flowing down the stream. As James crawled down the hill to her, his wounds on his arm had reopened and he was bleeding down the rocks to Blue Bonnet.

Slim and R.J. came galloping to the sound

of the screams as Little Red road away from them. The sight they saw was out of a horror movie, a long trail of blood lead down the rocks to a screaming horse trying to get footing in the red stained stream. James had reached the stream and was reaching for her, but she couldn't get to him. Her eyes were wide and horrified. Slim and R.J. crossed the stream to James.

"My horse, tend to my horse!" James pointed at Blue Bonnet.

Both men saw how much James was bleeding, looked at each other and knew what needed to be done.

R.J dismounted, grabbed a hold of James and wrapped his bandana around James' arm, "We will take care of your horse, but we need to stop this bleeding."

The men picked James up and put him on the back of R.J.'s horse, R.J. mounted.

Slim patted James boot, "I will stay with her til help comes."

R.J. was off in a flash to the homestead. James was bleeding steady now and he could feel his consciousness fading.

"Where did the stampede come from?" He leaned in so R.J. could hear him.

"Little Red…" is all R.J. said. It was all he had to say.

James began to lean on R.J., fading in and out.

"You are going to be ok, James," R.J. leaned back to tell him, "Don't worry, you aren't going to die on us."

James smiled, "I'm not worried about me R.J. The Lord saved me from the mountain lion and I believe he will save me from this, but if he chooses to take me home there is no better place to be."

R.J. thought with wonderment, "*How could*

*a man that is bleeding half to death, have such peace?"*

They finally reached the homestead and R.J. came galloping in yelling for help. Red, Pedro, and Susan all heard the yelling and came running. As they came out of the stable they saw R.J. sliding James off the horse blood dripping from James blood soaked bandages. They all rushed to them.

"Pedro! Go get the truck!" Red pointed and Pedro ran.

"What happened?" Red was breathing hard from running.

R.J. began, "Stampede…"

"Leg is busted. Passing out…" James interrupted and grabbed Susan's arm. "Take care of my horse…," his golden brown eyes focused intently on her and then he fell into R.J.s arms.

As Red and Pedro rushed off with James to the hospital, R.J. hooked up a trailer and Susan and he were off to save Blue Bonnet.

Susan's heart was pounding as they raced through the pasture on an old dirt trail. As they neared the corral, R.J. went off road towards the creek. When the truck slid to a stop, Susan rushed behind R.J. to find Slim standing beside the stream looking across it. He held up his hand for them to stop. Susan looked across the stream to see James' horse lying on her side breathing erratically. She was bleeding from a puncher to her side and rear leg.

"I tried to calm her and she nearly bit my arm off," Slim said smoothly.

"We will have to sedate her then," Susan opened her bag and got out the needle and three pressure bandages.

"You guys walk around her front side, I'll sneak around to the other side and inject her in the back." Susan knew a wounded horse could be very dangerous and that if she got in a vulnerable spot she could be kicked.

They began to move towards her, Blue Bonnet lifted her head, her eyes wild with pain. Susan made a long loop around and came in from the top. She eased down slowly as the cowboys started to move their hats back and forth. She reached down and stuck the needle in the horse and pressed it clean with one quick motion.

Blue Bonnet shot to her feet, pitching and kicking into the stream. She went about ten yards up the ravine and lay down. They steadily walked over to her as she passed out and fortunately for them she laid with her wounds up.

Susan pointed to her bag, "Get me that cleansing solution, Slim."

Slim ran over, grabbed the solutions, and brought it to Susan. Susan cleaned the wounds and applied the pressure bandages to stop the bleeding and promote clotting. They carefully wrapped a rope around Blue Bonnet's neck and used Slim's horse to drag Blue Bonnet unto an old blanket and then into the horse trailer. Slim and Susan stayed in the trailer with the horse while R.J. drove to the homestead.

Two hours had passed. James awoke to a familiar looking room and two rough looking cowboys standing beside his bed.

"My horse..." James blinked his eyes. His throat was dry.

Red grabbed James' foot, "Susan is taking care of her, don't worry."

James moved his arm and looked at his new bandage, "Did they fix me up?"

"Yep, said your leg was only bruised really badly, gave you a pint of blood and said you just needed to rest for a few days, but that you would be fine." Red encouraged.

"Take me to my horse," James struggled to

get up.

Red shook his head no, "The Doc said rest."

James reached for his hat, "I can rest with my horse."

"We'll ask..." Red stated with a frown on his face.

Susan had been working on Blue Bonnet all afternoon. She was worried that the bull had punctured her lung, but was relieved to find that the wound had not gone that deep. Susan treated the wounds for infection and applied new pressure bandages. Blue Bonnet's breathing had returned to normal. Susan was confident she would recover. Around seven o'clock Susan went and talked with Mr. Murphy.

"Any word on Mr. Montgomery?" She walked through the little white picket fence that surrounded the old farm house.

Mr. Murphy leaned back in his rocking chair, "No word yet, how's his horse?"

"She'll be o.k." Susan smiled and sat down in the chair next to Mr. Murphy.

"Good work Doc," Mr. Murphy smiled back, "You don't worry now. James will be alright. The good Lord doesn't make them any tougher."

Susan nodded and rocked in her chair, "Well, I am going to head home before it gets too late. I've sedated Blue Bonnet and she will sleep through the night, but I will be back early in the morning to check on her."

"We appreciate it, and drive careful," Mr. Murphy replied as Susan headed toward her truck.

She had already called Andrew and got a rain check on their date until tomorrow afternoon after church. Her mind was filled with concern over James. So much blood she thought... she prayed for his healing as she drove home. Susan wanted to rush to the hospital, but she restrained herself. After all she barely knew the man.

She recounted the story to her parents and they all prayed for James before bed. As she laid her head on the pillow she couldn't get the intensity of his eyes out of her head. In that moment when he had grabbed her arm, it was an onslaught of emotion. She felt fear, confusion and a strange sense of wanting to hold him. His eyes seemed to pierce into her very soul asking for help.

The next morning she arose before dawn, so that she could get out to the ranch and check on James' horse, then get back in time to get ready for church. She arrived at the ranch, walked into the stables to where Blue Bonnet was laying and what she saw overtook her. She opened the stall door. There was Blue Bonnet resting just as she had left her, but lying next to Blue Bonnet with his back against the wall and her head in his lap was James.

He was rubbing her nose real gently and looking down at her.

"Uhh Mr. Montgomery what are you doing here?! You should be in the hospital," Susan whispered as she quietly propped the stall door open.

He looked up at her with his golden brown eyes, "You can call me James. You took great care of her and for that I owe you my thanks."

Susan wasn't sure what to say. She had never seen such devotion to an animal, "How long have you been here?"

"Oh, a little while," James looked down at Blue Bonnet.

"Don't let him fool you Miss. He's been here all night." Red said standing behind her carrying some breakfast for James. "He convinced the doctor to release him last night. He should be in bed sleeping," Red shook his head.

Susan raised an eyebrow to James, "I'm

surprised your nurse let you go."

James just kind of grinned as he took the plate of food from Red, "She's not my nurse and besides it must have been her day off." James looked down at Blue Bonnet, "So she'll be o.k.?"

"We will have to keep her sedated for a couple more days, but she'll be fine." Susan assured, as she examined the wounds.

When Susan was examining the wound closest to James, he put his hand on hers, "Again, you have my thanks."

Susan felt something with his hand on hers, something she had never felt before.

"My pleasure," she smiled.

As Susan left the ranch she thought to herself, "*What kind of man leaves his hospital bed to sleep in stables with his horse and what was that feeling that had hit her with his touch?*"

She was able to get back home in time to

change and to make it to church a few minutes early. She noticed that the Murphys and Red hadn't arrived.

On the last hymn before her dad began to preach, she saw them come in the back with a limping James Montgomery.

Susan was floored, "*Was he crazy, he should be in bed.*"

After the service, she made her way towards him and noticed he was making his way towards her.

Susan walked to him and planted herself firmly in front of him with her feet together.

"You should be in bed, James Montgomery, what are you doing?" She asked in mothering concern.

James could see that she was still as breath taking as the day he first saw her, "Now I can't rightly leave the hospital for my horse and not come and worship my God, can I?" James held his hat in his hands.

"I suppose not," she was inspecting his bandages without touching him.

"So, I would like to thank you for what you did for my horse." James said plainly as he leaned on the side of the pew.

"You already did," she loosened her stance.

James looked down at her with a gentle smile on his face, "No, I mean I would like to take you to lunch today to say thanks."

"Uhh I... I would like that, but I have already made plans," Susan stammered.

James was not deterred, "Dinner then, tomorrow night?"

"Are you sure you will be alright, for that," Susan raised one eyebrow and pointed to his arm.

James grinned, "I can manage."

Susan looked down and thought for a moment.

"Then tomorrow night it is," she smiled.

"Let me get your number and I'll call you for directions." James stated.

Susan grabbed a bulletin, wrote her number on the back and handed it to James.

James took the bulletin and began to fold it, "Pick you up at 5:30?"

He slid the folded paper into his back Wrangler's pocket.

"See ya then," Susan looked up into those piercing brown eyes and smiled.

After church Andrew picked her up to go grab some fast food and play some miniature golf at Sparky's Put-Put golf. He had kept his word that it wasn't the same old dinner and a movie. As they set down to eat their burgers, Susan recounted the events of the weekend.

"Sounds like he really likes that horse," Andrew said after taking a sip of his coke.

Susan nodded, "It's more than that, he even made it to church."

"Well... good for him," Andrew said shortly.

Susan realized that she had been going on about James and that Andrew didn't care to talk about another guy on their date. There was a long silence and then Susan changed the subject. They finished their date and Susan couldn't help but feel bad that she had went on and on about James.

The next morning at the Triple 7 ranch R.J. and Slim were in Red's office explaining to Red how the stampede had begun. They went on to tell Red that when James rode off a little ways down to the creek, as they started to get the dust out for the cattle they noticed Little Red moving toward the gate. They figured he was just coming over to get more dust, but then the gate came open. Both men looked up as Little Red yelled as he ran around them "you better move."

R.J. and Slim just kind of stood their dumbfounded as little Red ran to the other side of the corral and fired his gun. The cattle immediately spooked and ran for the gate. R.J. and Slim ran away from the opening as the cattle poured out. When they heard James' horse screams, they both went to help, but saw Little Red riding off toward the homestead.

Red slammed his fist to his desk, "I can't allow that!"

Red waited for the men to come in for lunch and he took Little Red into the bunk house, "I know what caused the stampede, son."

Little Red looked to the ground, "Paw, I was just trying to scare him is all."

"I can't abide you no longer; you almost killed a man and his horse, not to mention endangering the cattle." Red walked down to Little Red's bunk.

Little Red watched his dad with a curious look on his face, "Paw, what are you saying?"

"You will always be my son, but as the foreman, you are off this outfit."

"What? You can't do this to me!" Little Red kicked a bed.

Red grabbed a duffle bag from Little Red's foot locker and tossed it on his bed.

"You did it to yourself son. Pack your things and go," Red turned and walked to the door. "Call your mother when you get settled," Red continued and then was gone.

Little Red stood there in the quiet dimness of the bunkhouse, with no one to whine too, no one to intimidate, just the very real consequence of very poor judgment.

Little Red left quietly mid afternoon with no idea where he was going or what he was going to do. About that time, Red was checking on James who was taking a little rest on the office couch. James awoke as Red entered the office.

"Aww I didn't mean to wake ya," Red slowly closed the door.

James could see that Red was distraught, "Are you alright?"

"I am sorry for the trouble my son has caused you," Red took off his hat and held it in his hands.

James sat up on the couch, "It's not yours to be sorry for."

"Well, I had to give him the boot.." Red trailed off with emotion. "A good foreman puts what is right before what is easy," Red regained his composer.

James stood up and put his hand on Red's shoulder, "I'll remember that."

Red nodded, and then went into his office. James slowly laid himself back onto the couch.

Chapter 9

The Thank You Date

Susan found herself nervous all day Monday and she just kept telling herself, "*It isn't a date. He just wants to say thank you.*"

Her dad was coming from his den into the kitchen and he noticed her pacing, "Another date with Andrew?"

She stopped her pacing and sat on the couch, "Umm, no, I am having dinner with James."

"The Cowboy?" Her dad inquired with amusement.

She nodded as if this was a regular occurrence for her, "Yes, the cowboy... He just wanted to thank me for taking care of his horse is all."

"Oh I see... Then why were you pacing?"

Her dad began to pace as she had been.

Susan laughed, "I am just ready to go, is all."

"Oh... Alright..." Her dad just grinned and went on in the kitchen.

James arrived on time despite the pain it took to press the gas pedal; wild stallions couldn't pull him away from this dinner. Susan had saved the only horse he had known as his own and he was going to make sure he thanked her properly.

Susan saw his truck pull up and she didn't wait for him to come to the door. She just yelled goodbye to her dad and was out the door.

James was a bit grateful to see her coming, because it was so painful for him to walk. He got out of the truck and slowly made his way to the passenger side. Susan slowed her stride as she watched this limping cowboy walk around his truck just to get the door for her.

"You don't have to do that, I know you are in pain," she called to him as she walked.

James never slowed his pace, "Not a thang."

She looked at him as she came around the truck; there was a smile on his face, but pain in his eyes. She got in and he shut the door.

As he made his slow journey back around the truck, she leaned over and opened the door for him. This took James by surprise, out of the women he had dated very few ever leaned across and opened the door for him in appreciation.

He slowly got into the truck, "So what are you in the mood for?"

"Oh, I don't care whatever is fine with me," Susan smiled.

James shook his head and turned off the truck, "That's not going to work. This is a thank you dinner and I aim to give you the meal you want."

Susan could see that James was not going to budge on this point, "Alright then... Umm, how about Mexican food?"

James started his truck, "Sounds great, now just tell me where to go," he motioned with his hand pointing in different directions.

They arrived at the local Mexican restaurant in town. They slowly walked to the front door because of James' limp. James opened the door and held it for her.

Susan thought, *"Opening doors must be something he just does."*

They sat down in a booth and ordered their drinks. James asked her what was good here and she told him a few of her favorite dishes. James looked over the menu as he spoke.

"So Susan, tell me about you," James looked deep into her with those eyes that invade her mind.

She looked down at the table, "Uh about me..."

"Yes," James nodded, "About you, like why you chose animals?"

Susan began to tell him about herself, the conversation just flowed between them. They laughed and talked all through dinner.

When desert came James started to pour honey over his sopapillas. "So tell me about this guy you are dating."

Susan looked around the room for a moment pretending to have to think about it, "Oh you mean Andrew?"

James finished chewing a bite, "I reckon if that is the ol' boy I saw you with the other night."

"Well, we have been on a few dates, but we are not boyfriend and girlfriend, if that is what you are asking," Susan looked right into James' eyes.

James shrugged and smiled, "I was just

asking who he was."

"Well, he is an associate pastor and works at an animal shelter," Susan continued.

"He's right up your alley then, "James grinned and grabbed another piece of dessert.

Susan nodded for a moment, "Yes, I suppose he is."

"How old are you? If you don't mind me asking," James took a drink of Dr. Pepper.

"Didn't anyone ever tell you, you aren't supposed to ask how old a lady is?" Susan raised one eyebrow.

James laughed, "I suppose I have heard that, but I seem to remember that applied to women who I figure would be quite a bit older than you."

Susan smiled, "Fair enough, I am 25, how old are you?"

"Twenty three," James folded his hands together on the table.

Susan sat back against the booth, "You're younger than me? No way!"

James nodded and grinned, "Sure looks that way, I guess now I will have to start calling you ma'am."

"You try it and the lightening will strike," she made a striking motion with her hand.

James crossed his good arm to pretend to block an attack, "No, I am good, I don't want any more of that!"

"What about you and Miss. Perky?" Susan tapped the table with one finger.

James looked bewildered, "Me and Miss. who?"

"You know, the perky little nurse I saw you with the same night," Susan said with a playful snotty tone.

James laughed, "That was just a onetime thing. I just wanted to thank her for the care she gave me in the hospital."

Susan raised her eyebrows and tightened her lips, "Oh so this is a regular occurrence for you to take women that have helped you out to dinner?"

"Well, if you consider two times a regular occurrence then ... Yeah," James smirked.

They finished their dessert and headed back to Susan's house, all the time talking about different things.

James thought to himself, "*This girl is really great!*" And Susan couldn't believe the kind of communication they were having.

"So, since I saved your horse's life and all..." Susan turned herself to face him in the truck.

James looked at her, "Oh brother here it comes. What do you want?"

She tugged on her seatbelt, "What was the other part of the thunderstorm reference in the hospital?"

There was a long pause, the longest in the night. James stared down the road as he spoke, "Are you sure you want to know?"

"I'm sure, I'm a big girl remember I can take it," she flexed an arm muscle.

James laughed, "Alright then, have you ever seen a thunderstorm rolling in over the horizon?"

"Yes," Susan replied, wondering where in the world he was going to go with this.

"I have seen many, being on the ranch all my life," James turned his truck down her street, "The air will grow stale and hot, everything will become very still, then a cool wind will precede it. You can see the deep blue coming toward you with lightening moving within the clouds. There are times when I think this is the most wonderful and beautiful of God's creations," James said as he stopped in front of her house. "So the first time I met you before I saw the lightening strike that you had, I saw how beautiful you are."

He looked over at Susan, her deep brown eyes full and wide, "And then you electrocuted me," James chuckled.

Susan snapped from her awe and laughed. "Well, all you had to do was take the Band Aid the first time I tried to give it to you."

James reached back into his wallet and pulled out the Scooby Do Band-Aid, "But I did take it."

Susan looked at him with wonder "You...You kept that?"

"Well, with my luck you never know when you're going to need one," James laughed and put the band-aid back into his wallet.

Susan laughed, "I suppose so."

James started to open his door and Susan stopped him by gently touching his knee, "I know your leg hurts, we can just say goodnight here. I had a wonderful time."

"I did too, and thanks again for my horse," James smiled as Susan got out of the truck.

"Oh yeah, of course, your horse," Susan had forgotten it was a thank you dinner.

James waved, "See ya' Sunday."

"Sunday," Susan waved back as she was walking to her front door.

James headed back to the ranch thinking it was too bad Susan was dating that Andrew fella. He felt so at ease with her and she was absolutely the kind of woman he would want to marry someday.

Susan closed her front door and just slid down against it. Her mind was spinning, "*James thought I was beautiful...He kept the band-aid... He made her feel like a lady...*" She was so at ease with him.

She talked to God silently, "Lord, I am so confused! There is Andrew on the one hand that has all the makings of a great man of God and wants to be a pastor. Then James on the other hand, who is a cowboy, rough neck, and gentlemen with all the makings of….," She stopped herself…, "Of a truly godly man."

She realized in that moment against the door talking to God, that Andrew was indeed a great guy, but there was just no cowboy in him. She smiled to herself knowing not too long ago that is what she thought she wanted, but now she could hear her mother saying, "Our ways are not His ways."

She continued to sit there thanking the Lord for his guiding hand, despite her stubbornness to look at the character of a man rather than his vocation. Now she wondered if James was the man for her or if he was just used by God to teach her a lesson.

Chapter 10

The Break Up

The next morning Susan was bright eyed as she came in to breakfast with her parents. Her dad had just finished reading the morning paper and was sipping on his coffee. Her mom was finishing cooking waffles and bacon.

Her dad looked over his coffee cup, "Did you have a good time last night?"

Susan sat down in her chair very proper, "As a matter of fact I did." She pulled her napkin into her lap, "It was a very nice thank you dinner."

Susan didn't want to rave about James as she did with Andrew; she needed to see where it was going first before she indulged in chatting about it.

Her mother made her rounds putting waffles

on everyone's plate, "Andrew called last night," she smiled and went back to get the bacon.

Susan poured syrup over her waffles, "Oh, did he leave a message?"

"He just wanted you to know he called," her mom unloaded the bacon onto their plates. "I just told him you weren't home."

Susan thought, "*I am going to have to address this and soon in all fairness to Andrew, but how do you say that you just aren't the one for me without someone taking it personnel?*"

Susan spent the morning in prayer about the situation with Andrew as she went about her daily vet duties of doctoring a variety of animals. She called Andrew during her lunch break and asked him if he would be willing to come to her house and talk a little while. Her mom and dad were going to dinner and she felt as if he deserved face to face communication. Andrew agreed to be there at six and as was his habit, he was there five minutes early.

Susan opened the door and waited on him to walk to her. He looked dapper as always, "Hey, Andrew," she gave him a quick hug.

Andrew hugged her back, "How are you, Susan?"

"I'm good... I'm good, "she held the door and looked outside, "Do you want to take a walk with me?"

Andrew nodded, "Sounds good to me."

They started walking down the sidewalk passing neighbors' houses and Susan swallowed, "Andrew, we need to talk about you and me." The temperature was still 98 degrees at six o'clock and they hadn't taken many steps when both of them began to sweat.

Andrew turned and looked at her as they walked, "O.K...."

Susan forced herself to look at him even

though she wanted to go invisible, "You are an awesome guy, I....I just don't think that you are the one God has for me."

Andrew looked from her to the sidewalk in front of them and after a long silence, "Something God has taught me over my few years, is that His plan is not always my plan." Andrew stopped walking, "You are a great woman, but I think when I find the one I will know she is the one." Andrew smiled at her, "We can still be friends, of course, right?"

Susan was in shock, "Umm... Of course!" She couldn't believe it was going this well.

*"God continues to show mercy to me,"* she thought.

Andrew turned on his heels; "Now can we get out of this heat, and you treat me to a glass of ice water?" He smiled.

Susan laughed, "You bet, the skies the limit

on ice water."

James slowly opened the door to check on Blue Bonnet. She was standing up eating a little hay. When Blue Bonnet saw him she came right over to nuzzle him. James fed her an apple, which she gobbled it up thankfully and he looked over her wounds.

*"She would be as good as new in a month or so,"* he thought.

He got her some fresh water, and then made his way to the office. He was still on restricted duty, by Red's orders and there was just no getting around that. As he walked toward the office he wondered when Susan was going to come out and check on the horses again. He found himself thinking about her a lot since their dinner.

On Thursday, Susan headed back out to the Triple 7 to check on Blue Bonnet. She was excited about this visit because it gave her another opportunity to see James. At breakfast Mr. Murphy had informed Red she was coming and Red mused to himself at the encounter he could orchestrate between James and Susan. Red and James were in their usual places in the office reviewing the things James already knew.

Red shuffled the papers on his desk, "Miss. Reddings is coming to the ranch today to check on your horse," he smirked. "I reckon you ought to be there when she is checking her out."

James lifted an eyebrow towards Red, "Hmmm... I reckon your right," James smiled inside.

"She'll be here around eleven," Red winked at James.

James just nodded and pretended he didn't know what Red was getting at, but the moment Red had said Susan was coming James heart went from a trot to a gallop.

Susan drove up a little before eleven and stopped her truck. She took a long breath as she looked around for any sign of James. When she didn't see him she headed for the stable. She had just past the entryway and was letting her eyes adjust to the dimness when she heard his voice.

James was standing by his horses' stall, "Good Morning, Susan."

Susan's eyes began to clear and she could see he was holding something, "Good Morning to you, James," she walked towards him, "What do you have there?"

James smiled, "Just a little appreciation gift."

Susan could see now that James was holding what looked like a dozen red roses wrapped in leather that looked to have come off of an old saddle bag. It was beautifully rustic and she loved it.

"These are for me?" Susan put her hand to her chest, "But you've already thanked me, James."

"Sometimes, one thank you isn't enough," James stretched them forward to her.

Susan took them in her arms, "They are beautiful, James, thank you!" She leaned in to hug his neck.

James bent down and gave her a big hug with his good arm, "I made a deal with Mrs. Murphy. These are from her personal flower garden."

Susan felt his strength in his arm as if he could just toss her to the sky. She held him a moment longer and then released him, "Oh? What kind of deal did you make?"

James straightened his hat, "I promised her that I would only give them away to someone more beautiful they there were," James smiled and looked down into her eyes.

Susan knees felt weak as she looked back

up to him, "Are you sure I fit that description?" She blushed.

"As sure as I am standing here," James opened his arms as to proof he was standing there.

Susan gained her composer, "Thank you so much. Now let's take a look at Blue Bonnet."

James propped open the stall door. Susan carefully laid the roses on the outside of the adjoining stall before going in.

Susan walked into the stall and looked Blue Bonnet over, "She is looking great."

"Wonderful!" James rubbed Blue Bonnet's nose.

"So am I going to see you on Sunday?" Susan removed the pressure bandage from Blue Bonnet's rear leg.

James looked over the horse at her, "You should know better than that. I'll be there."

Susan giggled, "Yes, I suppose I should."

She checked the wound for any infection.

"So when's your next date with the associate pastor?" James made his voice sound light hearted, but he really wanted to know how serious they were.

Susan stopped what she was doing and looked over the horse at him, "Well, the thing is... there won't be any more of those."

James put on a concerned look, but inside he was throwing fireworks, "Why? What happened?"

Susan began to take off the other pressure bandage by Blue Bonnet's chest, "This may sound a little extreme to you, but he wasn't the man God has for me."

James smiled, "That doesn't sound extreme, it sounds familiar," James began to brush Blue Bonnet, "But who would have thought it, he had all the right credentials."

"I know he did," Susan finished removing

the bandage, "But something God is teaching me is that His ways are not our ways."

James looked over at her again, "And you are sure the associate pastor isn't it?"

"As sure as you are standing there," Susan pointed to him and then leaned down pretending to check Blue Bonnet's wound again, "I am leaning more toward the cowboy type."

James stopped brushing. "I don't know if Little Red is available, but he might be," James grinned ear to ear.

Susan was quick enough to hit his hat off his head before he ducked, "You're asking for it cowboy," she giggled.

James walked around the horse to her with his hat in his hands, "So if I was to ask you out on a real date, how would you take to that?"

Susan walked to him and took his left hand in hers, she looked deep into him, "I would take to it very well."

James brought his right hand to meet hers and they stood there in an old stable stall and it was as the whole world faded except for them. As they stood there smiling at each other, the cowboy and the storm, love was whispered and both of them heard it.

Chapter 11

A Strong Witness

The men settled into their bunks after dinner and were telling cowboy stories, which many times were part fact and part fiction.

Slim sat on the end of his bed working his right boot off, "Well, I tell you one thing I don't miss, and that's Little Red."

Jose nodded and laughed, "Sí, sí, me no miss him either."

All the men started in on telling stories of the problems they had with Little Red, all of them except James Montgomery. He lay in his bunk with his right arm behind his head looked at the ceiling.

When R.J. came and sat on the bunk next to him, "I bet you are the most glad of all us that he is gone."

"I wouldn't say that," James leaned up to look at R.J.

R.J.'s face went into complete surprise, "The guy tried to kill you, James!"

James sat up, "Don't get me wrong, I am glad the danger is over," James smoothed out the bottom of his bed spread, "But that isn't the same as wanting the guy gone."

"What do you mean?" R.J. was perplexed by this and this conversation had drawn in the ears of some of the other men.

"You see, the Bible tells me that I should forgive because I have been forgiven," James took his Bible from his bed stand and held it in his hands.

R.J. looked to the bible and then to James, "Forgiven of what?"

"Sin," James looked at R.J. "The bible says for all have sinned and come short of the glory of God, which basically means we are all doomed to

Hell without forgiveness."

R.J.'s eyes were wide, "How do we get this forgiveness?'

James smiled, "We have to believe that Jesus Christ died for our sins as a sacrifice and that God raised Him from the dead. We then need to ask for forgiveness of our sins and for Jesus to come into our lives as our savior and Lord, and finally you need to tell people what you believe."

R.J. looked perplexed again, "Isn't there more to it than that?"

"There is more to living as God would have you live, but not more to salvation," James smiled.

As R.J. sat there looking at the bible, the lights went off.

"Everybody good?" Slim called out as he stood there next to the light switch.

"We're good!" Everyone called except James and R.J.

R.J. stood without saying a word and walked to his bunk to lie down. He kept his eyes open to watch James kneel and pray as he did every night.

On Sunday morning as James was combing his hair, he noticed a figure standing behind him in the mirror. James turned and it was R.J., his hair had been combed and he was wearing new wranglers and the nicest shirt he had.

R.J. held his hat behind himself with both hands, "I was wondering…" R.J. hesitated.

"Sure, you can come with us to church," James was a quick study

R.J. let out a long breath and smiled, "I'm ready then."

James smiled and put his hand on R.J.'s shoulder, "So am I."

R. J. was amazed at how pleased Red and the Murphys were that he was going with them. He had never been to church and before his conversation with James had no intention of going. R.J. had trouble sleeping all week and he figured there might be something to this if it was bothering him that bad. There was definitely something different about the kind of man James was and R.J. wanted to understand the difference.

They all entered the church at their normal time. Susan was at the piano watching the clock and looking for James. They both locked eyes as he walked in and deep smiles ran across their faces.

Pastor Reddings preached a powerful sermon on the Good Samaritan. R.J. felt like it was a good example of James. Near the end of the service Pastor Reddings started to talk about knowing Jesus and the life changing effect that it would have on you. R.J. listened to every word as if his very life depended on it. Then the Pastor asked if anyone wanted to talk about what he had said if they wanted

Jesus in their life. R.J. wanted to walk down the aisle, but a part of him held on to the pew.

After the service R.J. watched James walk directly over to Miss. Reddings and he noticed how her face lit up. The church people were all very nice and friendly. R.J. was surprised that he felt so at home here. The Murphys and Red were getting ready to go, so R.J. made his way over to James.

James was writing something on a piece of paper and quickly handed it to Miss. Reddings, "So when do you think I can get that by?"

Susan stuffed the paper in her purse and looked at R.J. walking up, "I would say by Tuesday, easy," she smiled at R.J. and James.

"They're ready to go," R.J. slowly walked up.

James smiled at Susan, "I am ready, bye Susan."

Susan smiled and waved as both men

walked outside.

"Have you taken a fancy to Miss. Reddings?" R.J. patted James on the back before they got into the truck.

James smiled and nodded, "I believe I have R.J," and they got into the truck.

R.J. was curious what Tuesday was, but he didn't figure it was his business to ask.

Tuesday morning came and went like the passing of a hot east wind. The men were just finishing lunch and heading out to their jobs when Susan showed up. R.J. was checking the tack on his horse when he noticed her truck pull up. As soon as it did, James jogged to her truck. R.J. was curious, so he slowly checked his gear and looked over to them a few times. He saw her hand something to James, they hugged for a second and then she was in her truck leaving. As R.J. was pondering what was in the package, he noticed James was coming towards him.

R.J. pretended to be very involved with his gear, out of the corner of his eye James was still coming.

"R.J." James called to him as he walked.

R.J. turned towards him, "Yes, sir... What can I do for ya?"

James reached him and stretched out the package, "No, it's what I can do for you."

R.J. looked at him in bewilderment, "Is this for me?" He took the package from James.

"Open it," James motioned to him.

R.J. looked at him a moment and then ripped the brown paper off the gift. He stood there looking at it, a black leather cover with gold lined pages, a Holy Bible. There at the bottom of the cover in gold was his name... R.J. Reeves.

"You didn't have to do this," R.J. was filled with emotion but held it shut. *"Miss. Reddings and him worked this out just for me,"* he thought.

"It is the least I can do. You have questions

and this book has the answers," James put his hand on R.J.'s shoulder, "Start with the book of John and if you have any questions, I'm here."

R.J. shook James' hand, "Thank you," and carefully loaded his Bible into his saddle bag.

"No thanks needed," James smiled.

The east wind kicked up dust around the men as R.J. rode away to his work and James walked on to the office.

Chapter 12

The Real Date




The request to get a Bible wasn't the only thing James and Susan had talked about that Sunday morning. He had also asked her out on a proper date for the coming Saturday night. She eagerly agreed for him to pick her up at six, but had no idea what they were going to do; only that James had told her to wear jeans.

James knocked on the door right at six and Pastor Reddings answered it. Susan had stayed in her room as to not to draw attention to her pacing.

"Come on in, James," Pastor Reddings welcomed him in, Susan had come out of her room so her dad didn't need to call for her.

James looked at her as if he had found a lost diamond, "You look beautiful."

Susan blushed, "Why, thank you kind sir."

"Well, umm, you two have a good time," her dad had never heard a man speak with such passion towards his daughter, it caught him off guard for a second.

James walked her to his truck and as was his custom, opened her door. Susan in turn leaned over and unlocked his as she had before and James just beamed. He started the truck and they were off to somewhere.

Susan shifted in her seat, "So where are we going?"

James turned a slight eye to her, "It's a surprise," and he focused back on the road.

"How about a hint?" Susan took the measure of James in as he drove. She had come to appreciate his character and now she took in just how handsome he was.

James looked over at her and back at the road, "A hint... Huh."

"Yes, please," she leaned forward to catch his eyes.

"A hint... A hint," James tapped his fingers on the dash thinking about how to give a hint, but at the same time not give it away, "The old west."

Susan looked up to the roof of the truck, "The old west? What kind of hint is that?"

"A simple one," James smiled, "and that is all you get thunderstorm or not."

Susan laughed, "Ok... Ok... The old west... Hmmmm."

As Susan was contemplating, James turned down the road going to the Triple 7 ranch.

"We are going to the ranch?" Susan looked at James with a big question mark in her mind. She hoped she was not going to eat with the men from the bunkhouse for their first date.

James pulled into the ranch and parked, "Come with me."

She followed him to the stables wondering what he could possibly have in store for her. As they entered the stables, there was Jose holding Blue Bonnet and another horse's reins. They were fully saddled and ready to ride.

"Oh a little ride before dinner, huh?" She nudged James.

James smiled, "Something like that."

James helped Susan on her horse, "You can ride, can't you?"

Susan mounted like an old pro, "Four years of riding lessons, I think I can manage."

James laughed, "Alright then, let's go."

The two of them headed out of the stables onto the South East pasture. The sun would be down in two hours and a gentle breeze cooled them as they rode. They talked and laughed as they headed into a wooded area. Streams of sunlight shot through the dimness and Susan was very cautious as they rode. After about a hundred yards the trees broke into a clearing and in the center of the clearing was a man and a horse. The man finished doing something as he saw them ride up; when they got closer she could see it was R.J. He had lit the citronella candles that were on stands at the four corners of a large blanket and in the center was a big picnic basket.

James looked to R.J. "Thank you."

R.J. just tipped his hat, "Anytime," and rode away.

Susan looked at all that had been laid out, she took in account the time it would take to plan such an outing and she was speechless as they dismounted.

James took her hand and motioned for her to sit down, "I know this isn't your traditional date, but I figured we could get to know each other better here, without all the distractions of other folks."

Susan gushed, "It's great!"

James started lifting out the plates of food already prepared. "Now this may not be gourmet dining, but in my opinion it is as close as you can get on the ranch."

Susan looked over all the food, "It all looks wonderful."

James reached for her hand, "Let's pray."

They blessed the food and began to eat. They talked about everything and nothing, laughing and flirting, sipping sweet tea and listening to the wind walk through the trees. The two of them were totally content in the moment with each other and totally captivated by the situation. They finished a special banana cream pie that Skillet had took all afternoon to perfect. Then James packed up the remains back into the basket.

He then laid down and looked up to the

night sky, "How long has it been since you took the time to look at the stars?"

Susan took her queue and lay next to him on the other side of the blanket, "You know, I can't remember the last time I really looked at them."

Susan would normally feel apprehensive about being alone with a guy in the woods at night, but she felt perfectly safe with James. The night sky was clear and the stars shone as if they had just been washed. With no invading city light to hinder their view, the site was quite spectacular.

They were lost in conversation for about two more hours when James told her it was time to leave. After pitching the remainder of the food away from the picnic area, James assured her he would tend to the rest in the morning. They both mounted their horses with ease and James produced flashlights to light the way.

When they arrived back at the stables Jose

was again waiting to tend to their horses. Susan believing the date was coming to an end waited for James to dismount.

"I have really enjoyed this." She smiled.

James eyes shinned like dark emeralds, "Oh, it isn't over yet, I still have one more surprise for you."

James reached for her hand and she instinctively took his. She followed him to his truck. As James got in on his side and started the truck he looked over at her with a smile.

"How are you at games?"

Susan looked over at him with an amused suspicious look, "What kind of games?"

"Hmmm, like charades," James lifted his dark eyebrow.

Her eyes sparkled, "I love charades, my parents and I play it whenever we can."

James headed out of the ranch, "Then this

will be fun for you."

They both chatted as James drove and Susan watched like a hawk for an idea of where they might be going.

*"Where in the world would we be going to play charades?"* She wondered until he turned down her road.

Susan adjusted in her seat to look at him, "My parents? You set this up with my parents?"

James just looked over at her and smiled a smile that he continued to hold even when they got inside. There were her parents waiting for them with the charades game on the table.

She was astonished that this idea would have even come to him, a daring move to involve the parents on a first date. Not to mention as she would come to learn, her clever mom and dad not saying a word about it all week, since James had set this up by phone on Monday.

Susan and James were on a team. She had never been so thrilled to be doing something so simple with someone. The night was a complete pleasure, they all laughed and talked and Susan and James both felt right with each other. At the end of the evening, James hugged her goodnight on the porch and was gone.

Her Parents stood inside waiting for their only child to walk back in the house. When Susan closed the door behind her, she didn't rant or jump up and down much to the surprise of her parents. She quietly walked to them with emotion in her eyes and hugged them both.

The Reddings stood there that night as a family holding each other in love. There was an overwhelming feeling that something special had happened that night.

Chapter 13

A Cowboy Meets Christ

James didn't get back to the ranch till nearly 1:30 in the morning. He turned off his truck lights as he made his way up the long dirt driveway and parked his truck. He was on his way into the bunk house when he noticed there was a light on in the office. This struck James as odd and he walked by the office window to see what the cause of it could be.

As he neared the window he saw R.J. sitting at Red's desk pouring over something and writing notes. James leaned up to the window and peered in, there on the table was the leather bible James had given him. R.J. was deep in study and James figured it better to just leave him be for now.

James crept into the bunk house as if he

was walking on air. He had just had the best date of his life with possibly the woman of his dreams and his ranch hand friend was studying the word of God. After thanking the Lord for his many blessings, James nestled his head into his pillow with a contented smile on his face and fell fast asleep.

The next afternoon James was sent to the livestock market to look at the quality of the other outfits and to see if there were good deals to be made. James thought this a perfect time to take R.J. with him so they could talk about God.

They entered the stands of the hot open arena; a quick west wind was blowing kicking up dirt devils on the floor of the arena. James and R.J. looked over a lot of the cattle presented; they weren't impressed with much on the market that day.

James crumbled the information flyer in his hand and looked over at R.J. who's eyes were fixed on the tan and white longhorns that were being presented.

"I saw you last night in Red's office, going over the Bible. I think that's great." James patted R.J. on the back, "Do you have any questions about what you were reading?"

R.J. stretched out his hand and looked at his fingers, "How do you know it's real?" He continued to look at his hand, "And not some fictitious tale like Zeus or Hercules."

James was taken off guard by the question; he had expected questions about what R.J. was reading, not deep philosophy from a weathered cowboy.

James swallowed, "Well, for one, we have first person accounts of Jesus in the New Testament. One of those is John that you are reading. We have the fact that the bible has remained for decades despite banning or burning, and the bible has never been proven false despite many attempts…"

"Pull your reins, there cowboy," R.J. smiled, "Let's take it one thing at a time."

James laughed and began to walk R.J. through the reasons he believed what he believed. The two men judged cattle as they were discussing eternal life. Finally, after about an hour, James stated matter-of-factly, "With all the reasons I have given you it still comes to faith."

R.J.'s eyebrow lifted and James continued, "Faith believes without seeing. Take the wind in the trees, I can't see the wind but I see the effects of the wind, it's the same with God. We all have the pull inside of us to find God. That is why you are up at night searching the Bible, because when your heart hears truth you know it."

R.J. was quiet for a moment, lifted his hat off and wiped the sweat off his head with his sleeve. "I need to think on this," came the final reply.

Both men were fairly quiet on the ride back to the ranch. James just figured it was best to let R.J. think through things, than bagger him with more information. They were midway down the dirt road that lead to the Triple 7 when James happened to look over and saw tears running down R.J.'s face. James immediately pulled over to the side of the road.

James put his hand on his friend's shoulder, "Are you alright?"

R.J. tried to compose himself to speak and it took a moment before he could, "Can you.... Help me know God?"

James smiled and opened up his glove box to reveal a Bible. He opened it to the third chapter of Romans and on an old dirt road in west Texas, James lead R.J. to the Lord.

James couldn't wait to tell Susan the good

news. In fact after thanking the Lord, she was his first thought. That evening he called her from the office and they ended up talking for two hours. Phone calls like this ended up being a regular routine for them both, every night, at least two hours a night. She couldn't wait to get his call and he couldn't wait to call her. They both found that the more they got to know each other the more they liked what they knew. Their going out on dates began to become a regular occurrence every week; they were drawn to each other. There was no mistaking what was taking place, love was blooming and everyone noticed.

Weeks ago, James had already come to grips with the fact that Susan had not been in his plans to own his own ranch. He understood very well that our plans are not always God's plans and he wasn't about to walk away from such a wonderful gift out of foolishness. James wanted to move their relationship to the next level; he wanted them to be exclusive to each other. He was pretty sure that was how it was anyways, however, they had never discussed it and he liked things set in stone.

One Thursday night, James couldn't stand it any longer as they laughed on the phone, he cut through the amusement, "I want to see you."

Susan's smile spread across her face. She was holding the phone to her ear with her shoulder as she worked on her nails. "I want to see you too."

"Now."

Susan took the phone in her hand, "Right now?"

"Yes."

"Where?" Susan had already stood up and was getting on her shoes.

James thought for a moment, "Meet me at the intersection of county line road 8 and 10. That should be halfway for both of us."

Susan looked around her room for her keys, "O.K, is everything alright?"

"Everything is great; I just want to see you." James voice registered affection.

"I am on my way," Susan needed no further reassurance.

"See you in 30," James added and hung up the phone.

His heart was pounding in his chest, "*O.K. big boy you have done it now… she might say no.*" His mind raced and he excused the thought because there was something between them that was perfect. He was in his truck before he knew it, driving toward his future.

Susan was checking her face in the rear view mirror as she drove, which she knew in her mind wasn't the safest of things to do, but this was an emergency. James had wanted to see her and couldn't wait. She felt she was the most desired treasure on earth and the feeling elated her to where she almost ran a stop sign.

These last couple of months with James had been glorious, she felt at home when she was near him and longed for his company when they were apart. He had been the perfect gentlemen and despite their many dates hadn't tried to kiss her. She thought how ironic it was that on her previous dates, with other men, those that she didn't want to kiss her tried to, and now that she has someone that she wants to kiss, he hasn't tried.

A strange sickening feeling hit her, *"Do I have someone, is James mine?"* Her mind began to over analyze, *"Have I jumped the gun again?"*

She turned down the road that led to the junction, she would soon see if he is hers or she has deceived herself. She checked the mirror again; the frown that had come across her face didn't help her makeup.

Susan could see headlights at the junction and knew it was James. It was very rare for much traffic to be out on the dirt road at 9:30 at night. As she drew closer she could see the silhouette of a broad shouldered cowboy leaning between the lights. She stopped her truck and they made their way for each other and they embraced as if he was going off to war.

James took her by the shoulders to look at her face, "I have something on my mind, and I need to say it out right."

James' face was serious with intent. A cold chill made Susan shutter, "O.K., go ahead."

"We have been dating for awhile now and we talk on the phone all the time."

Susan was losing patience, "Yes… Yes." She was nervous and didn't care to hide it.

James straightened as if he decided to

muscle his way through his thought, "I think we should be exclusive." He paused a moment as he looked at her wide eyes, "They used to call it steady."

"Steady," she repeated looking up at his handsome face.

James searched her face trying to figure out what she was thinking, "Yes… Steady, so what do you think?" James sharpened his eyes as if trying to peer into her mind.

Susan's face illuminated, "Steady sounds wonderful!" She threw herself into him, her face buried in his chest.

James held her tight smiling ear to ear, "This is great," he whispered.

Susan pulled back from him with the wry grin he had come to adore, "So do I get your varsity jacket or your senior ring or something?" Her eyes were dancing with amusement.

James tossed his head back and

laughed. "Ummm I don't have anything like that," he pulled from her relaxed arms, "But I do have this," James said as he turned and opened his truck.

"Oh, Honey, I was only joking," the word honey had slipped out so natural and after a second of doubt Susan figured it was fine. "You don't need to…"

James stopped her in mid sentence with his finger on her lips and he was holding something behind his back.

"Yes, I need to," he pulled his other hand around and opened it. "I thought of you when I saw this in town."

Susan looked down into his hand and laughed so abruptly that she covered her mouth, "A tire iron key chain, very… very nice."

The truth was she loved it, it was from him and he had been thinking of her. She took it by the chain and held it into the stream of a headlight.

"Better than the crown jewels," she gushed.

James took her hand and turned her toward him, his eyes showed love and she melted underneath the warmth of them.

She thought to herself, "*If you were ever to kiss me, kiss me now.*"

James saw the emotion in her eyes and a look of passion that flashed across her face. He bent his head to hers, she closed her eyes and their lips touched for the first time. They would never be the same again.

Chapter 14

Meeting the Parents

As another month past James became a
fixture at the Reddings house.   Susan's parents
thought he was a wonderful man and Susan herself
could not be happier.  James had asked Susan if she
wanted to spend Thanksgiving with his family and
she had been overjoyed at the request.  James called
and spoke to his family about their arrival, knowing
that he had never brought a girl home for any holiday.

James and Susan headed out to his family's
ranch early that Thursday morning, they planned to
spend the night and head back on Friday morning.

The ride didn't take near as long as Susan
had expected. For some reason, James' home had
always seemed to be a far off place. They started
down the dirt road that was the driveway of the

Montgomery ranch. Susan's eyes were wide with anticipation. She was nervous, she had only met his parent's briefly once before at the hospital. James spoke highly of his family and she really wanted their approval. She had no idea what their expectations would be. All James had told her was that they would love her.

James slowed to a stop in front of the house. Susan got out as the hot air hit her; she took a deep breath and looked at the home where James grew up. It was a small grey and white farm house with a big concrete front porch and a little picket fence that separated the front yard from the vastness of the ranch. James' mother came out onto the front porch rubbing her hands with a dish rag. She was a heavy set woman of medium height with black hair that time had peppered grey.

"Now ya'll come get in this house out of the heat," James' mother commanded in a sweet voice.

They both took strides toward her. Susan waited as James gave his mom a huge hug and then lowered his head for her to kiss it. His mother turned to Susan.

"Welcome to the Montgomery's, dear," and gave Susan an unexpected hug, "Lunch is almost ready; ya'll come in here and relax."

They all went into the house and James took a quick look around.

"Where is dad and Grandpa Bean?" James turned to his mother.

His mother went right to the stove to check the turkey, "Your dad is out checking on the herd and grandpa is probably piddling somewhere."

James left to bring their bags into the house while Susan asked if she could help with the food. After James' mother gave an approving smile, she put Susan to work cutting vegetables for the salad. Susan's mother had taught her long ago how important it was to ask to help in the kitchen if you were a guest.

"Where do you want me to put these?" James asked his mom as he held Susan's bag and his.

James' mom turned from the stove only for a moment, "She can sleep in your old room and you can sleep on the couch."

James went to deliver the bags, "Sounds good, Mama."

The steam from the boiling water on the stove was filling the kitchen. James' mom opened up the one window she could and turned on a box fan. With the sound of the fan and the boiling water Susan didn't hear James' father and grandfather come into the room. She had a feeling she was being watched and turned to see the two men looking at her as James was telling them something. They all grinned the same. Susan wiped her hand off and turned to extend it to his Father. Mr. Montgomery saw her coming and rubbed his hand down the side of his leg to make a vain attempt of cleaning it before shaking hands.

"It is a pleasure, Susan," Mr. Montgomery took her hand and shook it carefully.

Susan smiled big, "The pleasure is mine, sir."

She noticed that he had the same eyes as James. Susan reached for James' Grandpa's hand.

"You bet, welcome," is all he said when he shook her hand.

The two older cowboys went off to wash their hands as James sat down and the two ladies began to put the food on the table. When they were all seated at the table and holding hands, James did the honors to bless the meal.

Susan wondered if James' mom always cooked like this. If she didn't, she had surely outdone herself.

James' mom took a few bites and then directed her attention to Susan.

"So how did you two meet?" She looked from James to Susan patiently waiting for a reply.

Susan smiled and told the story starting with her flat tire. Everyone at the table smiled, nodded, and listened until she got to the part of the stampede where James went into the hospital.

Mrs. Montgomery turned her eyes to James with lines between her brows, "Hospital? We didn't get a call," she made the statement, but James knew it was a question.

James held up one of his hands as if he was slowing traffic and swallowed the food he was chewing.

"Now, mama, I was only in there for about five hours and then they released me. That old mountain lion wound just got reopened is all."

Mrs. Montgomery laced her fingers together

on the table and turning her eyes from James to Susan.

"If that happens again you make sure he calls us," she smiled at Susan.

Susan without hesitation, "Yes ma'am, I will."

She felt elated that James' mom saw her being in his life to call them.

"Let me tell you what else your son did," Susan grinned a wry grin. James just let out a defeated sigh.

Mrs. Montgomery's eye brows rose, "Oh, do tell."

As Susan recounted her seeing James in the stall with Blue Bonnet both his dad and grandfather went to laughing.

Mr. Montgomery smiled at his son, "Nothin like a good horse,"

"Nothin," Grandpa Bean reiterated and took

a sip of his sweet tea.

After dinner the men helped clear the dishes and then went in the small living room to watch the Dallas Cowboys battle against the Washington Redskins. The women decided to go ahead and wash the dishes before they joined the men.

Susan was washing while Mrs. Montgomery was drying and putting the dishes away.

"I sure like your home," Susan scrubbed the bottom of a pan with an SOS pad.

"The Lord has blessed us with it," Mrs. Montgomery was putting the glasses in the cabinet.

Susan looked around as she scrubbed, "I bet all the girls James has brought here have loved this place."

Mrs. Montgomery turned from the cabinet with one eyebrow lifted. She walked over and put her hand on Susan's shoulder and leaned close to her ear.

"James has never brought a girl home

before you." she quietly whispered.

Susan's eyes widened and she looked at Mrs. Montgomery who had a deep and thoughtful look on her face.

"I reckon that makes you special, Hun." Mrs. Montgomery smiled, winked and turned back to drying towels. Susan continued to wash dishes but her spirit was on cloud nine.

After the football game they all went out to play horseshoes under two extending shade trees. Mrs. Montgomery had no desire to play so she was made the official referee. Susan had played horseshoes only once or twice in her life, but she was a good sport and willing to give it a go. Grandpa Bean had been pitching for 50 years so he took Susan as his partner. Susan and James were next to one stake and Grandpa Bean and Mr. Montgomery were at the other. As the game went on Susan and Grandpa Bean were winning despite no help from

Susan.

She looked over to James as they waited for the opposite side to pitch, "Why do you call your grandpa, Grandpa Bean?" She smiled.

James laughed, "Well, back when the depression hit, he and my grandma fell on some hard times as most people did. She was a frugal woman and had saved cans and cans of ranch style beans."

James stopped a moment to pitch his horseshoes, "Anyways, those beans are what they ended up eating for a couple months and needless to say, my Grandpa was tired of beans. He was working for the Bar Y Ranch back then. Apparently, one day he made the statement to some of the cowboys that there was no way he was going to eat another bean, because if he did he would surely turn into one. He was going to make it clear that his wife needed to figure out something else."

James laughed to himself and shook his

head, "So the next day one of the cowboys asked what he had for dinner the night before. My grandpa took off his hat, looked down at the ground and said....beans."

Susan smiled and looked at Grandpa Bean who was sighting in his next ringer. James breathed in deep with humor, "So from then on they called him Cowboy Bean and that transferred to Grandpa."

That evening after supper everyone sat around on the porch and talked. Susan and Grandpa Bean touted their victory and everyone was in high spirits as bedtime rolled around. Everyone said their goodnights and James waited until Susan had closed her bedroom door to make his way to his parent's room. He gave a quiet knock and his dad opened the door for him to come in.

James sat at the end of the bed looking back and forth between his mother and father who were just smiling and looking back at him.

"Well?" James finally let out.

His mom nodded, "I really like her James. She has a good heart and helped me in the kitchen."

James smiled and looked to his dad, "Dad?"

His dad grinned, "Well she can't throw horseshoes to save her life." They all laughed, "But I tell you son, she looks at you the way your mother looks at me and that is saying something."

They both hugged him and James snuck back to the couch with excitement in his heart. He loved her and his parents liked her. It was time to start thinking about the future which is exactly what he ended up doing half the night.

The next morning after breakfast Susan and James were headed back to the Triple 7. Susan was pleased to hear that his parents liked her. Her parents had already given James a big thumbs up weeks ago and she couldn't be happier about it. As they drove they started talking about topics that had never come up before, like how many children they wanted, how they wanted to raise them, where they wanted to live, etc. The more they talked the more they realized that they didn't agree on everything, but they did agree on the important things.

Chapter 15

A Hospital Call

It was the middle of February on the Triple 7 Ranch. The holidays for James and Susan had gone by so quickly, but they sure had been wonderful. The ranch was still as busy in winter as it was in summer. The men had to set out hay and supply water when the creeks froze over. James had continued his routine of office work in the morning and ranch hand work in the afternoon.

It was a cold, dreary day when James and Red past through the doorway to the office, Red closed the door behind them, then stumbled a little too quickly to find his way to the couch.

James turned at the commotion and saw that all the blood had seemed to drain out of Red's face. He was clutching at his chest and James knew he was having a heart attack. James didn't hesitate, he rushed out the door and yelled to R.J. and Slim before they road off to their pastures. Red wasn't making any sounds, however the pain in his eyes spoke volumes as the three men carried him to Mr. Murphy's suburban. Then rushed Red to the hospital, as Slim drove R.J. and James prayed over Red and kept him talking.

Hours had passed since they got him admitted and there was no word yet on his condition. Three rough looking cowboys sat in the waiting room with hats in their hands watching the minutes drag on like days.

Red's wife, Mrs. Lansdale, had come and was sitting with the men doing her best not to break down into tears. The doctor finally made his appearance after another thirty minutes had passed. He stood in front of the cowboy's and Mrs. Lansdale with his hands behind his back as if he was able to give a lecture at the medical school. As the doctor began to speak Mrs. Lansdale took James' hand to brace herself for the news.

The Doctor swallowed deep, "He's alive and in stable condition." The doctor paused to let the relief wash over his audience. "Mr. Lansdale suffered an acute myocardial infarction commonly referred to as a heart attack."

The Doctor looked at Mrs. Lansdale, "There are some life changes he is going to have to make, and after he is rested I would like to go over them with both of you."

Mrs. Lansdale nodded, "When can I see him?" Her eyes full of tears.

"You can go in now, but he is resting, so don't wake him." The Doctor smiled.

They all sat with him as he slept for another hour and then James sent Slim and R.J. back to the ranch. Mrs. Lansdale and James both wanted to be there when he woke up. Another hour past and Red slowly opened his eyes. He saw James and his loving wife sitting on either side of his bed.

Red cleared his throat and they looked up at the sound, "I'm still here, Honey." He gripped her hand as she held it tight with both of hers and put her head down to it.

Red could feel her tears tracing down his hand as she closed her eyes.

James took the other hand and smiled at his old mentor, "Between the two of us I think Triple 7 should get a discount."

Red smiled underneath his bushy mustache and then became serious, "So, heart attack?"

His wife raised her head with a look of determination, "Yes it was, Red." She drew her eyebrows together; "The doctor says you are going to need to make some life changes."

Red smiled at her serious look, "No need for

the stern face, my love. I will do what they tell me I need to."

Red looked to James, "I am going to miss my fried foods."

James chuckled, "Maybe we can get Skillet to cook cholesterol free meals."

They both grinned at that idea.

"Not likely, since his main ingredient is butter." Red let out a little laugh and looked around his room, "Well, do they feed you in this place for heart attacks? I haven't eaten since breakfast."

Mrs. Lansdale stood and wiped her cheeks, "I'll go ask them what you can have." Red nodded and she was out the door.

Red turned to James and gripped his hand, "All kidding aside, thank you for what you did today."

James just shrugged, "No thanks needed, sir."

Red gripped his hand tighter, "No, James, there is thanks needed. I reckon you saved my life today with your quick decisions."

James just smiled, "You are welcome, sir."

Both men had been so involved in the conversation that they hadn't noticed the figure standing at the door. Little Red was holding his hat his face full of emotion. He felt a small hand touch his back and move him forward as his mom slipped in beside him. She motioned with her head for Little Red to go on in, as he moved both men turned to see him.

Red blinked his eyes, "It is good to see you son." He opened his arms and Little Red came into them.

James stood up and whispered to Mrs. Lansdale, "I am going to give ya'll a minute," and she nodded with approval.

James found his way to a vending machine

and sat down in the waiting room with his treasures. After about thirty minutes Little Red came out into the area James was in and headed straight for James. James sat up in his chair, not sure what Little Red was up to.

Little Red came and stood before James as men used to stand before kings. He looked to the ground and then to James.

"I have no doubt you saved my Paw's life, he lives a good one unlike me," he swallowed and shifted his weight in his boots. "I did you wrong on more than one occasion. I'm a no good bandit and I want you to know I am sorry," he stood for a brief moment, and then turned to walk away.

"I had already forgiven you," James stood and watched as Little Red turned around.

Little Red shook his head, "Why... Why would you forgive me?"

James smiled and looked straight at Little

Red's eyes, "Because God has forgiven me."

Little Red looked away as if what he heard had physically hurt him. He tipped his hat to James and disappeared through the shaded hospital doors.

Chapter 16

The New Foreman

Red spent a few more days at the hospital before he was able to come back to the ranch. He had gave James full run as acting foreman. Mr. Murphy and Red spent the remainder of the week rocking on the porch talking.

On Saturday morning they called James to come and sit with them. James sat on a bench and leaned his back against the wall; the two older cowboys rocked in their chairs and stared out into the pasture as they talked.

"How is the day to day business going?" Red rocked back in his seat as he spoke.

"Going great, our cows won't calve until April and we have plenty of provisions for the livestock through the rest of the winter," James moved his shoulders against the wall finding a place to rest them.

Mr. Murphy coughed, "You had any trouble with the men?"

James raised an eyebrow, "No sir."

The old cowboys stopped rocking and looked at each other and then turned to look at James.

"We have been talking and we feel it is time for me to pass on the saddle horn," Red smiled big as he sat up in his chair. "We want to make you foreman."

Mr. Murphy just smiled and nodded as Red spoke. James sat upright and looked at both the men in amazement.

"I am going to head over and take me a rest, while Mr. Murphy gives you the particulars on your new income and so on," Red stood up and shook James hand, "I will still be around if you run into a jam and need some seasoned advice." He slapped James on the shoulder, "I couldn't ask for a better replacement."

James held back his excitement and smiled at Red, "I had an excellent teacher."

Red just waved the complement off and went toward his quarters. James would discover later that Mr. Murphy had set Red up with a retirement package that was unheard of for a cowboy.

Mr. Murphy motioned for James to sit in the rocking chair. They spent the rest of the afternoon discussing what was expected of him and his salary.

James invited Susan to dinner that night to give her the big news. After arriving at the steakhouse Susan looked at James with questioning eyes, for if there was steak to be eaten they always went to the ranch. James had only told her that he got big news today and wanted to tell her in person.

As they sat she couldn't wait any longer, "Well, what is the big news?"

James placed his hat next to him on the seat, "You are looking at the new Foreman for the Triple 7 Ranch!"

Susan reached up and grabbed his hands, "Aww, Honey, that's great! Tell me everything."

James recounted the events of the afternoon and Susan listened with great interest. As James finished telling her the rest of the story, Susan noticed that a cloud hung in James' eyes.

Susan looked into his eyes as only she could, "Is something bothering you about all this?"

James looked down at their hands intertwined and then looked at her, "I don't know if I am ready for the responsibility of such a large ranch." He moved his thumb over hers.

Susan sat back and looked at him. She had

never heard doubt in his voice before and it was a strange sound to her.

"James Montgomery," she said in an assertive voice, "You are the strongest man that I know and God has made you what you are, so trust in that."

At that moment it occurred to Susan that for the first time in her life a man had superseded her father in her eyes and she knew she wanted to marry such a man.

James took her words to heart and the cloud over his eyes vanished. He was ready to be James again.

"Well, I guess my first act will be to bring my vet in from mom and dad's ranch," he smirked.

Susan smiled because she knew he was just trying to rile her up, "Oh, you are, are you?"

"Unless you think that's a bad idea," James was trying not to smile.

Susan sat up a little in her seat and let her eyes flicker a little flame to him, "I think it is a great idea. Not sure how good of a date that new vet will be though."

James laughed, "Old Tucker isn't much for going out," James looked at her with amused affection, "So I reckon I had better stick with you then."

Susan smiled and gave James a knowing look, "Well, if you think that is best for the ranch."

James put his hand to her cheek, "It is best for the ranch and definitely best for me."

Susan leaned her cheek into his hand and both of them let out a sigh of comfort.


James had rolled into the foreman position as if he had done it for years. He had long ago earned the men's respect and the ranch was doing well. However, when he should be at complete contentment, he was having trouble sleeping.

James found himself thinking a lot about his future with Susan. He loved her. James knew he wanted to make her his wife, but he wanted the timing to be right.

He started taking midnight walks to talk to God and seek his guidance. On one of these walks he heard footsteps behind him. He turned and it was R.J. walking to him.

R.J. cleared his throat, "Are you alright?"

James shuffled his feet, "Yeah, I am just talking to God about Susan."

R.J. nodded, "You mind if I ask about what?"

James had come to know R.J. as a great friend and they often talked of the Lord, "Well, I want to marry her and I am not sure if this is the right time to ask her." James took off his hat and rubbed his head, "What do you think I should do?"

R.J. looked up to the stars, "You know I haven't been a Christian near as long as you, but it seems to me when God gives you a gift you accept it." R.J. turned to look James in the eyes, "It is just like salvation. You don't question the gift you just accept it in faith."

James smiled and put his hand on R.J.'s shoulder, "When did you get so wise on spiritual things?"

R.J. smiled back at him, "It's all God, brother, and I had a good friend guiding me."

James patted him on the shoulder, " Well, I figure I will need a best man for this deal, and I know no better man to fill that position than you."

R.J., who wasn't one to show emotion unless talking about God, let the emotion be heard in his voice, "It would be an honor."

James put his arm around his friend as they walked back to the bunk house. "Now we need to discuss how I am going to propose."

Asking for Susan's hand in marriage was something that James didn't consider lightly and he believed in the tradition of asking her Father first for his blessing.

James made his way to the church one Tuesday morning when he knew Susan was busy working at her clinic. He saw that Pastor Reddings' car was in the parking lot and he knew today was the day. He slipped into the church and made his way down the hall to the Pastor's office. The door was open, but James knocked on the door frame anyways and waited with his hat in his hands to be called in.

Pastor Reddings immediately looked up from his study, "Well, this is a surprise, come in and sit down." James did as he was instructed, "Is everything alright, James?"

James nodded, "Yes sir, everything is

great.... I have come to talk to you about Susan."

As soon as Pastor Reddings heard this he figured what was about to take place, "Alright son, what's on your mind?"

James took a long breath, sat up straight and looked the Pastor square in the eyes, "Well, sir... I have come to ask for your blessing to marry your daughter."

At this Pastor Reddings stood up and walked around the desk to James.

"James you're a good man who follows the Lord and my daughter loves you. I can think of no better son-in-law to have. You have my blessing."

James stood up to shake the Pastor's hand but instead he found himself in a hug.

"Thank you, sir...Now that we have that squared, there is a favor I would like to ask of you."

Chapter 17

The Proposal

It was late march when Susan received a phone call from James asking her to meet him at the Triple 7 Ranch for their Friday night date. She thought it was a little odd, since James always picked her up from her house. But maybe he was tired of driving all that way every week, so she just went with it.

Susan arrived at the ranch around six o'clock and was amazed to find it was a virtual ghost town. Not even Mr. Murphy was on his porch. James' only instructions were for her to be there at six and to meet him in the stables. Susan figured they were going to take a nice ride in the coolness of spring.

As Susan entered the stables she was

surprised to see that James was not there. However, in his place was R.J. dressed very nice in a black hat and holding the reins to a saddled horse.

Susan approached him smiling, "Hey R.J. where's James?"

R.J. didn't say anything, but instead handed her an envelope with her name written on it in calligraphy. Susan looked to the envelope, then back to R.J. who just nodded for her to open it. It was sealed with wax with the Triple 7 brand. She was careful to open it and remove the letter. It simply stated: *Follow the Lights*. She looked back to R.J. He handed her the reins, tipped his hat and pointed to the opening on the other end of the stables. As soon as Susan took the reins, R.J. walked away. Susan wondered what James was up to and was anxious to see what he had planned.

She mounted and started out the direction R.J. had indicated to find a path in the middle of torches showing her the way. As she rode she felt the coolness of the late afternoon and the smell of spring filled her lungs.

She had ridden far enough to where she could barely make out the homestead behind her. She noticed ahead of her in the distance a silhouette of a cowboy also in a black hat. Beyond him the lights were no more. As she rode closer she saw that it was Mr. Murphy smiling as she came.

Susan eased up to him and said, "Hi, Mr. Murphy."

Again her only reply was an envelope handed to her; the same as before with her name on the front, sealed with the brand.

Susan quickly opened it to find more instructions. *Dismount, take what is given to you and patiently wait.* She looked to Mr. Murphy who nodded, so Susan dismounted. When she did Mr. Murphy reached into a bag he had tied to his saddle horn. He pulled out a clear glass vase and exchanged the vase for the reins in Susan's hand. Mr. Murphy tipped his hat and rode off leading her horse beside him.

Susan stood there between the last of the torches looking around her, amazed that James got Mr. Murphy involved in one of his dates. James was always surprising her with creative dates. This seemed to her that it was going to be the best one yet.

Susan heard a distant rumbling that could have been thunder. She looked to the sky, except for a few clouds, it was clear. She turned to look at the sun and thought to herself that she had about an hour before sunset. The rumbling came closer. Susan could tell it was coming from in front of her, about three hundred yards away was a gentle sloping hill and she couldn't see beyond it. The rumbling came closer and closer. And then over the hill she saw cowboy's hats moving up and down. They reached the top of the hill and stopped. All of them lined the top of the hill and faced her. They were all wearing black hats, except the cowboy in the middle who was wearing a white hat. Susan guessed this must be James and thought, *"That boy he went all out on this one."* As she stood watching the hill, she quickly counted all the cowboys. There were fourteen in all, which she knew was half the ranch had on hand.

She watched with anticipation as the cowboy on the end farthest to her left took out across the plain between them, galloping straight for her. He pulled up just short of her and she realized she didn't know him. He looked down at her, tipped his hat and pulled a long stem red rose from his saddle bag. He carefully dropped it into the vase she was holding and rode away toward the homestead. As soon as he started away from the other end of the cowboy line rode another cowboy. It continued like that... cowboys with long stem roses, taking turns from each side of the line riding to her and then vanishing.

After one of the cowboys rode away, Susan looked with anticipation for the last cowboy in the black hat to come, but he didn't take off like all the others did, he sat waiting beside James. It was only then Susan realized that she had a dozen roses in her vase.

"What does this next rider have for me," she wondered.

She saw James' white hat nod and the rider took off toward her. When he reached her, she smiled. It was R.J. again. He must have circled around her to be with the other men. He leaned down and handed her another envelope. Susan quickly put her vase down next to the pole of the torch and took the letter from R.J. He tipped his hat, as all of the men before him, and was gone.

Susan looked at the envelope, then at her

man in the distance in the white hat. She carefully opened it and again the letter was simple: *Walk forward and sit in the chair.* Susan looked ahead of her and around her. There was no chair in sight; however she did as she was instructed. She picked up her flowers and began to walk forward.

As soon as her feet began to move she heard a horse coming to the right of her. She turned to see a rider coming carrying a high-backed chair. He rode about fifty feet in front of her and dropped the chair so that it was facing the rider in the white hat. Then he continued riding in the same direction. Susan watched as James slowly walked bluebonnet toward her. He got within 50 yards, then stopped and leaned on his saddle horn. A moment later, from the colors of sunset five men she didn't know road up and surrounded her. Susan sat very still and waited to see what was about to happen. They began to sing a harmony about love, life, and God. Through the harmony Susan heard a familiar voice among them singing from behind her. She turned quickly in her seat to see her dad all dressed in cowboy attire singing with tears in his eyes. Susan's heart began to pound.

*"This was not some fancy date,"* she thought, *"Her dad was here, this is big."*

The men finished the song, Susan turned to look at her father who winked at her and rode away with the other men.

As Susan turned back to look for James, he had already riding up and was dismounting. His boots hit the grass and Susan took full sight of him, a new Stetson hat, a white pressed long sleeve shirt, black wranglers, and white boots. She had never seen him so dressed up. She gripped the vase of flowers as her hands began to tremble and then sat them down so she wouldn't drop them. James walked towards her, smiling as only he could at her. He reached for her hand and she immediately gave it and rose to her feet. He didn't speak. He just turned her to the west and walked a few feet, then pointed to the horizon. Susan had been staring at him and had been so caught up with what was taking place that she didn't notice that the sun was about to set. The sky was beautiful with streams of pink and purple clouds ushering in the evening stars.

The sun had just touched the earth when James turned her towards him. His eyes full of emotion as he looked into her awe struck face.

"I have never known a blessing from God that equals you. You are my heartbeat, and I love you more than life itself."

James took off his hat and went to one knee. Susan's eyes filled with tears. She stood with one hand over her mouth and the other in his hand.

James raised his left hand, "I have already put on the ring you gave me."

Susan looked at his left hand and wrapped around his ring finger was the Scooby do band aid she had given him the first time they met. She couldn't believe he had kept it this long, tears rolled down her cheeks.

James reached into his pocket and pulled out a box.

"Susan Marie Reddings, will you marry me?" James opened the box and before her was the most beautiful diamond ring she had ever seen, this ring was especially for her.

Susan whispered through her tears, "Yes, I will marry you James Morgan Montgomery."

He slid the ring on her finger and rose to embrace her. She hugged him as hard as she could. He picked her up and swung her around as if she were as light as a cloud. James gently put her feet back to the ground and kissed his future wife with all the love he had in him.

Chapter 18

A Wedding Day

With all the preparation the months before the wedding had flow by. James and Susan both agreed on having a small wedding. They were amazed at how much was involved with the planning and coordination. Susan wanted the wedding at the Triple 7 ranch since that is where there first real date was and her proposal. The Murphy's were delighted by this decision. They left no stone unturned to make the ranch a candle lit, tree trimmed, wedding wonderland. The most beautiful piece of acreage on the North Pasture was chosen for the event. James made sure the cattle were kept off of it and the grass was watered and finely cut.

Susan was going to wear her mother's wedding dress for something borrowed. She bought ivory heels for something new and at James' request her bouquet was of blue bonnets for something blue.

Her dad had volunteered to perform the ceremony. Pastor Reddings and his daughter had a serious conversation on if he was going to be able to get through the wedding without breaking down in tears. Finally, James was the deciding factor when he announced that Pastor Reddings was his pastor and he didn't want anyone else to marry them.

Most people don't get married outdoors in November it is way too cold, however in Texas it is just entering fall.

It was a cool midmorning with a gentle breeze carrying white fluffy clouds and the dew on the grass sparkling in the sunshine. The little field they had picked was framed with trees in a horseshoe fashion. The grass had been so well taken care of it looked like a golf course. Chairs were set up as to make an isle in the middle and everything was beautiful in white and gold.

Cowboys under cowboy hats and women in summer dresses lined the chairs. An acoustic group was playing a soft melody. James stood next to the white arch way adorned with bluebonnets. R.J. stood next to him, both of them in black hats, tux tops, black wranglers and black boots.

Susan and her mother were in a white canopy tent putting the finishing touches on the bride.

Her mom put her hands on Susan's hips and looked over her shoulder into the mirror, "Is something wrong with the dress, hun?"

Susan wiggled a little in the dress, "No, mom it's perfect." Susan looked back at her mom in the mirror, "Mom, do you think I'm ready?"

Susan's Mom smiled, "Yes, honey I do."

"All I know of about being a wife has been

watching you and you seem to do it with such ease. I worry sometimes that it might not come so easily for me."

Susan's Mom turned her daughter to face her, "Susan, no one knows going into marriage, how to be married. It's something you learn along the way. If you seek the Lord and his guidance he will help you come to be the wife you should be."

She hugged her daughter, "You are a fine woman and you will make a wonderful wife, I love you."

Susan's eyes went cloudy, "I love you too, Mom, thanks."

Susan's mom nodded, "It is time honey, are you ready?"

Susan took one more look in the mirror, "I love James with all that I am, I am ready."

Susan's dad was waiting outside the tent to lead her down the aisle, give her away, and marry her and James.  Pastor Reddings allowed himself the briefest moment of reflection, his only child, his little girl, and his princess.  She was soon to be a wife, no longer under his roof or in his care, memories of her as a little girl sprang forward in his mind and with them tears flooded his eyes.  He stopped the tears immediately, James was a great man, a blessing from God and Pastor Reddings was going to do this ceremony right.  He straightened and felt the soft arm of his daughters slip into his.

The acoustic group began to play Here Comes the Bride and all faces turned to the woman in the white flowing dress.  As Susan and her father began to walk down the aisle, she looked at a few faces that were all looking at her adorningly.  Her heart was pounding a mile a minute and she could feel herself begin to sweat. She looked toward the front to find James, his face beaming with love, Susan was instantly at peace.  Her father gave her away, then switched roles and began the ceremony.

James and Susan listened intently, as Pastor Reddings spoke of keeping God first, encouraging each other in love and being devoted. They were both nervous and both realized how important this moment was. Susan and James meant every word of their vows and took great joy placing the rings on each other's finger. They kissed and were presented as Mr. and Mrs. Montgomery, Susan had waited her whole life for such a title and it was more than she ever thought it would be.

After all the cutting of the cake, the shaking of a million hands and all the parts that comes with a reception. James and Susan left under a blanket of rice in his old pickup truck with coke cans tied to the bumper. They were heading to their honeymoon and a huge feeling of relieve passed over both of them. They were married, it was done. James pointed out the window to the distance horizon, to a deep blue sky and storm clouds forming.

"You know I was wrong about comparing you to the beauty of a storm," James reached and took her hand. "I have never seen anything as beautiful as you."

Susan blushed and smiled, "What about comparing my temper to a storm?"

James gave her the grin she loved, "Naa, I was right on about that."

And both of them laughed the cowboy and the storm.

The Cowboy and the Storm©2008 Kirk Mann

The Cowboy and the Storm©2008 Kirk Mann

The Cowboy and the Storm©2008 Kirk Mann

230

Made in the USA
Charleston, SC
02 December 2011